THE AMISH WIDOWER'S PROMISE

AMISH WOMEN OF PLEASANT VALLEY BOOK 3

SAMANTHA PRICE

AMISH ROMANCE

PROLOGUE

YEARS HAVE PAST since Book 2. Read on to learn what has happened to the people of Pleasant Valley in the past three years.

Rebecca is nearly nineteen, a trainee midwife, and still expects she'll marry Dean ... someday.

Mary is married to Samuel Kauffman, and together they have Lois, Mary's secret child from her previous marriage to her late husband, Damian. Mary and Samuel have been praying for more children.

Karen and Jason—the bishop's nephew

and Rebecca's cousin—now have twin one-year-old boys. Karen is happy, but exhausted most of the time trying to keep up with them now that they are crawling and trying to walk.

Bishop Elmer and his wife, Hannah, have thirteen children, of whom Rebecca is the only girl and the second eldest. Their youngest child, Andrew is now four, and their oldest, Timothy, is twenty.

Marilyn, the community's midwife, is training Rebecca to take over from her one day.

Mona, raised in Pleasant Valley, has returned with her husband, Jacob Raber, after nearly ten years living in his community. She's heavily pregnant and has chosen to give birth to their first child where she considers home.

CHAPTER 1

"I DON'T MIND TELLING you it hasn't been easy. It's double the trouble and twice the work."

Rebecca smiled at Karen's baby boys whom she'd helped deliver one year and two days ago. "They are beautiful and adorable."

The twins, Casey and Caleb, crawled off in separate directions. It seemed Karen and Jason had their work cut out for them.

"You must be nearly ready for the next addition to the family. Perhaps another set of twins, maybe triplets? Hmmm?"

Karen laughed. "Are you trying to drum up more business?"

Rebecca giggled. "Now that I'm nearly a fully-fledged midwife I need some business. Not that I'd ever charge you, not after everything you've done for me."

"Oh, the room? It was nothing. I had the money with that unexpected inheritance and after I bought my home I still had more left over. I can't think of anything better I could've done. I never had a *schweschder* to spoil." Several years ago, Karen had given the bishop money to build on a bedroom specifically for Rebecca, to save her from having to share with her younger brothers. It hadn't been easy for Rebecca living with twelve brothers in a four-bedroom home. Thanks to Karen, for the last four of those years she'd had her own bedroom.

"I'm surprised *Dat* accepted the gift." Rebecca would never forget Karen's kindness.

"I talked him into it. I can't imagine what

it was like for you sharing a room with three of your brothers." Karen winced. "Not in your teenage years."

"I had no privacy at all. Even when they were supposed to be asleep there was one of them always awake, always wanting me to tell him a story so he could drift off to sleep. It changed my life when I got a decent night's sleep and didn't have to watch over the boys and fetch them water in the middle of the night or accompany them to the bathroom in the dark."

Karen gave a little giggle. "That's what it's like when you've got children of your own."

"I probably won't have to worry about that."

"What do you mean?"

"Midwives never marry."

Karen threw her head back and laughed, and stopped when she had to jump to her feet to rescue a coffee mug from one of the twins who was trying to get it off the coffee table. "I'll have to step up the security around here. They're doing more and more every day."

"Reaching further than ever, I see."

Karen sat back down. "Now what's this nonsense about midwives not marrying?"

"Marilyn never married. It's just not the lifestyle that's conducive to marriage."

"That's not so. Many midwives marry."

Rebecca raised her eyebrows. "Name one that you know of."

Karen breathed out heavily. "I'm sure there are. It's just the midwives in this community didn't marry and it's not something that should become a pattern. *Gott* wants everybody to marry. That's how he designed us—to want a spouse. Don't you want love?"

"I guess so. *Jah,* I do."

"What about Dean? What does he have to say about your single-life pledge?"

Rebecca thought back to her childhood friend and neighbor. She'd grown up thinking she'd end up marrying him and she was sure he felt the same. There hadn't simply been a silent understanding, they'd even talked about it when they were ten and agreed on it. Since then, though, nothing had happened. Dean might not even be interested in her anymore, but she knew for a fact he'd never gone out with any other girl. "I guess I'll probably marry him, if anyone, but he's never asked me on a buggy ride or anything."

"I wouldn't worry about it. It's just a matter of time."

"Do you think so?"

"Of course. You suit each other perfectly."

"I guess so. But it just feels 'blah' when I think about marrying him." She poked out her tongue. "You know? I want it to be how it was with you and Jason. I knew that first day you met there was something between the two of you. Sparks flew through the air like fireworks on a dark night."

Karen put a hand over her mouth and giggled. "I do admit there was an instant attraction. I felt something."

"I honestly just don't feel that will happen for me. If I was married and cooking dinner with several *kinner,* what would I do if a woman went into labor?"

"You would leave off and go to the birth and then come back. The whole family would have to look after themselves, or someone would have to fill in for you. You'd have something in place for those times. The woman in labor has to come first."

"Exactly—that's what I mean. And isn't family supposed to come first?"

"Not when you're a midwife and you have people relying on you."

"Can you see where I'm coming from?" Rebecca asked. "It's a conflict."

"It's not as though you became a midwife later in life. Your husband would have to understand that's just the way things are and he'd marry you with that understanding. And you'd always have someone on stand-by to help your family if your husband couldn't take over."

"So, what I'd have to look for is an understanding man?"

"Exactly."

"And have you met any of them lately?" Rebecca's face twisted into a smile and Karen laughed at her.

"You're so mean, Rebecca."

"I'm not. I just think that most men are pretty selfish. That's what I've seen and that's what has been my experience in the three years I've been helping Marilyn. I don't think the wives get enough sympathy from their husbands when they're giving birth."

"I guess most men feel pretty helpless when that's going on."

Rebecca shrugged her shoulders. "I suppose that might be it."

"You never know what's going on in someone's mind. Your *vadder* told me that."

"*Jah, Dat* is full of wisdom. He's always got an opinion on everything."

"And so he should; he is the bishop after all."

"*Denke* for reminding me, but that's something I could never forget." She glanced at the wooden clock on the wall. "I'm going to Mary and Samuel's when I leave here. Mary has a woman there for me to meet. Her name's Mona and she's come back to this community for Marilyn to deliver her baby. Marilyn's meeting me over there."

"What's her name? I didn't catch what you said."

"Mona, and Jacob is her husband. I don't know their last name. I think she was from here originally, but he's from somewhere else." Rebecca jumped up and rescued one of the twins who was trying to stand and nearly toppled over.

. . .

REBECCA LEFT Karen and traveled to Mary's house. More than anything Mary had said she wanted another child. She already had four year old Lois, and had been married to Samuel for nearly three years and still hadn't conceived.

Mona was only a couple of weeks away from her expected delivery date. And in Rebecca's experience, delivering two to three weeks either side of the due date was normal. The baby could arrive any day.

As soon as Rebecca knocked on the door, Mary opened it and grabbed her by the arm. "Marilyn called and said she's can't come out. She has a slight cold and didn't want Mona to catch it."

Rebecca knew she could handle this on her own. Marilyn would retire one day, and she'd be flying solo when that day came. It was time to have a practice run. Besides that,

Rebecca had a sneaking suspicion Marilyn really wanted a rest. It wasn't the first appointment she'd missed of late. "Okay."

As Mary showed her into the living room, Rebecca reminded herself how much experience she'd gained over the last two years, trying to bolster her confidence. She'd delivered many babies by herself, but Marilyn had always been there in the background.

Mary introduced her to Mona, who was sitting upright and looking uncomfortable. Rebecca leaned down and shook her hand. "Pleased to meet you, Mona." Mona was a pretty woman, small, with delicate features.

"*Denke* for coming. I would like to meet Marilyn, too, before the birth."

Rebecca noticed Mona's cheeks were red and she didn't look well at all. "How are you feeling, Mona?"

"Not too good. We had a long journey today and it's taken it out of me."

"What you need is a good rest," Mary said. "You can go to bed whenever you're ready. Don't feel you have to sit up and make polite small talk. You're here as our guest. I'll have Freda bring dinner to your room."

"*Nee,* I'm not that bad. I'm fine."

"Have you met Marilyn before?" Rebecca asked.

"*Jah,* do you remember me? Oh, you probably wouldn't. You were just a child when I left the community to marry Jacob. Jacob is from Holmes County," Mary explained. "I knew Marilyn back then."

Mary said to Rebecca, "Mona moved away ten years ago to marry Jacob and it turns out he's a good friend of Samuel's."

As they drank tea, the ladies talked some more.

"Are you married, Rebecca?" Mona asked.

Rebecca placed her teacup back into the saucer balanced on her lap. "*Nee.* I was just talking with one of my other friends about marriage. Being a midwife is not conducive to being married. Marilyn's never married."

"What you need is a good man, who will make you forget you're a midwife and remember you're a woman."

Rebecca giggled. "That's something like what Karen, my friend, said. And then we joked that I wouldn't be able to find a *gut* man." When she saw Mona didn't find it funny, she explained, "An understanding man can be hard to find. It was just a joke. Probably a mean one. I shouldn't have said it. It probably wasn't nice."

"My Jacob is very understanding."

"I'd like to meet him, then. I mean, does he have any brothers?" Rebecca joked.

"He has many brothers, but unfortunately they're all married."

"It seems the good ones are." Rebecca laughed and then when Mona remained stony faced, she told herself never to make a joke around Mona again. She was taking everything way too seriously.

"Rebecca, aren't you marrying Dean?"

Rebecca gasped and stared at the mischievous sparkle in Mary's eyes. "Don't start with me, Mary."

Mary giggled.

"What's this about Dean?" Mona asked, perking up a little.

"He's just a boy that I always figured I would marry. We grew up together and he was on a neighboring property, and from the time I was a young girl I realized the man I would marry would be amongst the community. I used to look at all the boys and guess which one he'd be. I guessed Dean. It just made sense, you know?"

"You're so lovely you deserve a good man," Mona said.

"Oh." The unexpected compliment from a stranger made Rebecca notice heat creep into her cheeks. She secretly hoped that someday a man would have the same opinion of her that Mona had expressed. *"Denke,* Mona."

"Nee, I mean it, Rebecca. How about I find you a man who's truly worthy of a woman such as you?"

Rebecca stared at the mother-to-be, who apparently had no sense of humor. "I wouldn't want to move from this community."

"When you're in love nothing else matters except to be with the one your heart desires. You'd go to the desert with him and live under a palm tree. Wherever he is, that's the only place you want to be."

Rebecca pushed away the image of living in the desert, and thought about being in love. She wanted a love like Mona described, a love all-consuming and complete. Someone her heart could be hungry for. "Okay. Please find someone if you think you can."

Mona's lips turned up at the corners just slightly, and it looked as though it took a great effort to do so. "And, will you keep an open mind if I name someone?"

What did Mona mean by that? Would he be old, or ugly? "I guess so." Rebecca hoped she wouldn't live to regret those words.

"Then I will … when I have given birth, I'll find you a lovely man who's worthy of a beautiful young *maidel* such as yourself."

Rebecca gave an embarrassed giggle. She hadn't been complimented like that in quite some time.

CHAPTER 2

WHEN REBECCA HAD BARELY GOTTEN into to bed that night, her pager sounded. Her father, having the authority as the bishop, had allowed midwives to have pagers for their emergency calls.

She looked down at the screen and recognized the number as Mary and Samuel's. She slipped her feet into her boots, and hurried out to the barn to call them back. She guessed Mona had gone into labor.

"Hurry, Marilyn's on her way already."

"Mona's in labor?"

"Jah, didn't I say that? And far along from the noises she's making."

She didn't like the panicked sound in Mary's voice. She was usually calm; nothing ever bothered Mary too much. "I'll be right there."

Her father came toward her holding a flashlight. "Do you have to go?"

"Jah, Mona's in labor."

"I'll hitch the buggy. You go inside and get yourself ready."

She looked down at her nightgown, her stockingless feet in her untied boots, and laughed. *"Denke, Dat.* I appreciate your help."

Her father didn't sleep much and was always there to help on those middle of the night rushes to get to her birthing mothers. Maybe this 'understanding man,' wherever he was, would also help her hitch their buggy so she could get to the births speedily.

A NIGHT and a day had passed and now they'd hit the twenty-four-hour mark. Jacob turned over the washcloth on his wife's forehead. They were heading into the danger zone and Marilyn had whispered to Rebecca that she'd shortly suggest again that Mona be taken to the hospital.

Overhearing, Jacob told them Mona had given strict instructions she didn't want a doctor, or paramedics, or any medical intervention. Mona had told Marilyn her doctor had given her the all-clear for the usual homebirth that the Amish favored.

Rebecca noticed that some women handled pain better than others. Marilyn always told them not to think of what was happening in their body as pain, and to replace it by feeling their body opening to allow the baby to come through. It helped most

women, but some—in the throes of labor—
told Marilyn she wouldn't know what it was
like because she'd never given birth. Which
was a valid point. Rebecca was certain she'd
make a better midwife if she had been
through that process. Maybe someday ... Rebecca's mind was snapped back to the
present when she heard Jacob.

"Try to keep calm please, Mona."

"I need to push," she said.

Marilyn gave Rebecca a relieved look and
she knew Marilyn had been wondering how
much longer Mona could've taken the pain.
Two minutes later, Marilyn was pushing and
Mary came back into the room. Half an hour
later, a baby boy was born.

"It's a boy," Mary called out excitedly.

"Is there life?" Mona called out, with fear
in her voice.

"*Jah,* he is well," Rebecca said to relieve
her mind.

Mona gave a deep sigh and relaxed.

Marilyn cleared the baby's airways, and handed him to Mona. "You have a beautiful *bu* and everything is fine."

"That's all I ever wanted." She looked up at Jacob. "I might not live to see him grow up."

"Don't be silly," he answered.

Rebecca was trying to give them as much privacy as she could and so were Marilyn and Mary, who'd moved to the other side of the room.

"I'm dying," Mona said.

"You aren't, Mona. Everything is fine." Jacob leaned over and kissed her forehead.

"I am dying," she whispered to Jacob. "I had a dream."

A chill ran down Rebecca's spine when she heard those words. Joseph's dreams in the Bible had come true, and the fearful look in Mona's eyes spoke volumes.

Jacob whispered back, "Everyone dies, my love, but you're not dying today or any-time soon."

Mona smiled and she stared down at the baby as she ran her hands all over his body. "Look at our *wunderbaar bu,* Jacob."

"He is beautiful, and so small."

Marilyn began fussing about doing the clean-up, ordering everyone about as she normally did.

IT WAS another baby Rebecca had helped de-liver. There was no greater joy than helping bring a life into the world. She and Marilyn would routinely check in on their new mothers every day for the first week to make sure both mother and baby were doing well.

EVERYTHING WENT WELL with Mona and the baby until two nights later when Rebecca got an urgent beeper call and was asked back to Mary and Samuel's house.

Mona had a raging temperature and had refused to go to the hospital. When Rebecca and Marilyn arrived, Mary, Freda the house-keeper, and Jacob were doing their best to get her temperature down. The windows were open and they were sponging her down with cool wet washcloths.

When Marilyn showed Jacob his wife's temperature on the thermometer, she told him, "It's dangerously high."

"Your call, Jacob," Mary said, wiping her forehead with her arm as she held a wet washcloth above the bowl of cool water.

"*Nee*," Mona called out.

"I know you want to abide by her wishes, but she could die if we don't get help," Marilyn whispered.

He gave a nod to Mary. *"Jah,* make the call."

Mary wasted no time leaving the room while Rebecca said a silent prayer that Mona would be okay. She'd never before been in an emergency situation such as this and she hated seeing Mona in pain and thrashed about. Rebecca squeezed the cold water out of the washcloth and wiped Mona's face again, trying to keep her cool.

"I'll get some more cool water," Freda said before she hurried out of the room.

"I need the bathroom urgently," Marilyn said.

Rebecca nodded and now she was alone with Mona and Jacob.

Mona reached out, grabbed Jacob's arm and raised her head. "Jacob, when I die promise me you'll take another *fraa.* Micah must have a *mudder.* All I want is his happiness in this life. You need to find a *gut* woman."

"You're not dying, Mona."

She looked into his eyes. *"Gott* is calling me. I had that dream. I can hear the angels singing. Jesus is coming for me."

Rebecca could only look on in horror. Was the woman experiencing some delusional state that came with high temperatures? Or is this what happened when people died? She prayed for the paramedics to be faster.

"Jacob, promise me you'll marry again." When he remained silent, she said, "My last request is that you promise me you'll marry …" Mona turned her head and looked directly into Rebecca's eyes. "Promise me you'll marry Rebecca." She gasped and closed her eyes.

"Don't talk, Mona," he said. "Someone do something," he yelled, and then he gave Rebecca a pleading look.

Rebecca started wiping down Mona's

arms, wishing Freda would hurry back with more cool water.

Mona opened her eyes again and raised her head to look at Jacob. "Will you do this one last thing I ask? For me, for Micah and for ..." she struggled to breath and held her chest in pain.

"I will, I will," he said.

Her head fell back onto the pillow, and Jacob looked on helplessly as Mona heaved out a large breath and closed her eyes.

She was gone. Rebecca knew it and so did Jacob. Tears fell down Rebecca's cheeks. She'd never been with someone when they'd died.

"Why did she die?" Jacob asked. "Why?" He looked up as though he was talking to God. Tears rolled down his face.

Rebecca was wiping her own tears when Marilyn rushed back into the room.

"What's going on, Marilyn? Why did she

die like this?" Jacob's voice was filled with anguish.

Rebecca shook her head and stared at Mona, and then Freda came back with a bowl of iced water. Then, seeing what had taken place, she set it down on the dresser. They all stood in silence as Mary walked back into the room.

"They're on their way," Mary said.

"It's too late," Jacob said. "It's my fault. I should've said to call them sooner."

"It was her choice, Jacob," Marilyn said soothingly. "She didn't want medical help."

MINUTES LATER, everyone left Jacob alone with Mona, while Micah continued peacefully sleeping in a crib in the next room.

Just outside the bedroom, Marilyn quietly said, "I should've asked her—and Jacob—many more questions, Rebecca. She came here just days before she was to give birth.

She gave me no idea of her medical history and I never should've agreed to this."

"You think she had an illness?"

"We'll know more soon," Marilyn said to the sound of the ambulance sirens. "Never forget this, Rebecca. Always make sure you know and verify a woman's medical history." She shook her head. "She must've had a prior condition."

"It's not just the flu or something like that? An infection from the birth?" Rebecca recalled her clutching at her heart and struggling to breathe. "Maybe a heart problem?"

"She had a bit of a heart murmur, but said her doctor told her it was okay." Marilyn shook her head. "It can't have been an infection. I mean, it's not likely. The placenta was whole and complete, none was left behind. It's unusual to have a high fever and die from it after childbirth. I suspect there's more going on that we don't know about."

Rebecca looked around and saw Mary

being consoled by Samuel in the hallway, and young Luke, the live-in stable hand, was patting Freda's arm.

THE NEXT HALF hour was a blur for Rebecca. She had walked to the living room and slumped onto the couch. Then she overheard some loud conversations.

"What's going on?" Samuel asked the paramedics.

"We don't know much at this stage. Did someone say she just had a baby?"

"That's right. Only two nights ago."

"Maybe infection set in."

"She already seemed like she wasn't feeling well before that," Marilyn said.

One of the paramedics said, "Where has the husband gone?"

"I'll take you to him," Marilyn said.

Once Mona had been taken out of the house, Rebecca found herself unable to move. She heard a buggy, got slowly to her feet, and took two steps to the window. It was her father. Of course. Someone must've called him.

Freda walked over to her. "Are you okay, Rebecca?"

"I don't know what I am. I can't believe she was alive, and now she's gone so quickly. And … it's so tragic with the *boppli*, and all."

"I know. I should get back to the kitchen and make everyone a hot drink. Would you like to help me?"

"*Jah.* I need to do something and right now my head's all a muddle."

Rebecca had never been around such a tragic event and she felt such a heavy sense of sadness in the air as she followed Freda into the kitchen. "I can only imagine how Jacob must be feeling."

"And everybody who witnessed it. It's such a sad thing for the child to be without a parent."

Then Rebecca remembered what Mona had made Jacob promise. At least when he'd agreed, that had given his wife some comfort in her last moments on earth. She wondered what her father would say to comfort Jacob. "Mona is at home with *Gott,* but now the child has to grow up without his *mudder,*" Rebecca mumbled.

"Just don't say that in front of Jacob. He already feels bad enough."

Rebecca shook her head. "I won't say a word. I would never ..."

FOR THE NEXT couple of hours, Rebecca kept busy doing everything she could to make things easier on everyone in the household. Marilyn had already offered to stay the night to help with Micah, the young baby.

. . .

Dawn was breaking as Rebecca traveled home alone in her buggy. Until now, she had been pleased about becoming a midwife and delivering children into this world. Now she felt useless. If only she could have stopped Mona from dying.

Rebecca had never been so close to death. Her grandparents on both sides were still alive and although many people in the community had died, she had not been close to any of them. Of course she had known it would happen one day.

The moment when she'd watched Mona take her last breath came flooding through Rebecca's mind. Then a chill went down her spine again as she remembered the promise Mona's husband had made, and the intense way Mona had looked into her own eyes. It was an awkward thing and she wondered if Mona truly believed her husband was supposed to marry a woman much younger, someone whom he barely knew, just so the baby could have a mother. Sure, in time he might marry again; most youngish widowers married a second time.

WHEN SHE GOT HOME, her mother came running out to meet her and Rebecca collapsed crying into her mother's arms.

"Leave the horse for your *vadder* when he comes home."

"*Nee*, I'll do it." She dried her eyes and stepped back. "I'll be in soon."

"I'll wait for you in the kitchen."

Rebecca unhitched the buggy and then rubbed down her horse before she let him loose into his yard. Placing one foot ahead of the other, she trudged into the house.

"What happened?" her mother asked once Rebecca was in the kitchen.

"It was dreadful. Did *Dat* tell you why he was called?"

"*Jah*, he did. They said Mona died."

"That's right."

Her mother put a comforting arm around her and walked her to the table. "Sit down. I've heated you some soup."

"*Denke.* I forgot how hungry I was. I didn't even eat."

"You always forget to eat."

According to her mother, she forgot everything. "We still don't know why she died. She had a high temperature and that's all we know."

"And the *boppli?*"

"He's perfect; he's a perfect child." She didn't tell her mother the awkward thing Mona had made her husband promise. There was no need to mention something as embarrassing as that.

"I wonder what the poor man will do now? He'll have to go back to Holmes County without his *fraa.*"

"And he'll have the new *boppli.*"

"Oh, the poor man."

"Poor Mona, and poor infant." Rebecca sighed. "Oh, *Mamm*, I don't know if I can do this again. I think every time I deliver a *boppli* I'll think of Mona."

"She didn't die in childbirth. You must do this again. Everyone's relying on you. Marilyn's not getting any younger and we need you to take over."

Her mother placed a bowl of steaming soup in front of her. "You were against me being a midwife from the start."

"That was a long time ago, and since then I can see how dedicated you are. I was wrong to discourage you, it seems. You give up your food, your sleep, and all your free time to look after the women and bring life into the world. I'm proud of you. There are not many women who would do that."

"I would think there would be a lot of women who'd do that."

"There aren't. Marilyn has taught you everything she knows."

"Not everything."

"Experience will teach you the rest. You have to put this behind you; I don't think anything like this will ever happen again."

Feeling sick, Rebecca put her hand over her tummy. "It doesn't matter. It did happen and I can't get past it."

Her mother shook her finger at her. "You can and you will. *Gott* will help you. You have to develop strength and determination. That's what's missing in young people today."

"Stop please, *Mamm.*" Rebecca put her fingertips to her forehead. "You're beginning to sound just like Aunt Agatha."

"Maybe you need to speak to Aunt Agatha."

"*Nee,* I don't. I just need some rest, and a good night's sleep tonight, and then I'll probably be okay."

"I'll let you sleep in tomorrow morning, and you just rest for today. I'll have the boys do your chores tomorrow and the next day."

Rebecca nodded. *"Denke, Mamm."* She sipped a spoonful of soup, pleased to notice it helped with her nausea.

"I will be staying around the *haus* until your v*adder* comes home."

"He might be a while."

CHAPTER 3

THAT NIGHT, Rebecca couldn't sleep. She gave up trying when it was morning and the sun was climbing into the sky. After she showered and dressed, she walked into the kitchen to see her father sitting at the table having breakfast.

"How long did you stay there last night, *Dat?*"

He adjusted his round thin-rimmed glasses. "I've only just returned."

She slumped into a chair and saw her

mother fussing around at the other end of the kitchen.

"*Kaffe,* Rebecca?" her mother asked.

"*Jah,* please."

"Breakfast?"

"*Jah,* anything." Rebecca turned back to her father who was eating pancakes with syrup. "How's Jacob?"

He shook his head. "Not good."

"I feel so awful for him. I just wish I could've done something."

"It was her time," her father said.

Rebecca nodded and knew her father had to say things like that. Maybe it was true, or maybe something could've been done. It didn't seem right that God would want to take a mother away from a child.

As though he knew her thoughts, he said, "He knows the beginning from the end. We only know our own narrow viewpoint."

"What do you mean?"

"Sometimes people die to save suffering."

That could be right if what Marilyn suspected was true, that Mona had some kind of illness.

"You have no appointments today, do you, Rebecca?"

"We had one, but Marilyn told me she'd make a call and move it to next week. It wasn't urgent. I'll visit Mary and see how she is. Do you think I should go back there, *Dat?*"

"I think you would be very welcome."

IT WAS STRANGELY quiet at Mary's house. Mary opened the door looking as though she'd had no sleep. The two women sat in front of the fire while Lois played with her wooden toys on the rug.

"Mary, how did it happen—have you heard?"

"We're waiting to hear back from the hospital."

"In all the time I've been helping Marilyn,

I've never seen anything like this. Marilyn thinks that she had some pre-existing condition that she didn't tell us about."

"Don't worry about any of it now. We have to be strong, so Jacob ...."

Rebecca nodded and fought back tears.

"The funeral is arranged for Friday."

"That's six days away. It's Saturday today." She counted up on her fingers.

"I know. Mona didn't have many family at Holmes County and most of her relatives are here in Pleasant Valley, so it makes sense to have the funeral here."

"Where's Jacob?"

"He hasn't come out of his room. The *boppli's* in the room with him now. Marilyn fed him in the middle of the night and then Jacob insisted on taking over. I think Marilyn is still asleep."

"I wish I could've slept."

"Me too."

THE NEXT DAY was Sunday and Rebecca thought maybe she would find out what was going on.

Rebecca saw Jacob outside the Millers' house, where the meeting had just finished, and he was holding the baby close to himself.

She walked over to him. "How is he?"

He smiled at her and then glanced at his baby. "He's beautiful."

"He certainly is."

He took his eyes off the baby and looked at her. "Do you remember my promise to Mona?"

She nodded. "Something like that is hard to forget." She thought he would say to forget it, and was unprepared for the next words that proceeded out of his mouth.

"I suppose we should get to know each other first."

Was he joking? She smiled and looked at

him, thinking that it was somewhat odd to joke about his wife's misguided last request. Then she saw by his solemn face he was serious. *"Nee.* You didn't take it seriously, did you? I mean, we can't marry."

"I gave my word to my *fraa.* And I take that seriously." He gulped.

"You made that promise, *jah,* but I had no say in it. You can't make someone promise something like that. I'm young but even so, I know that."

"You haven't married anybody yet. Do you have someone in mind to marry?"

She did. It was Dean, the handsome Dean who lived close to her. "It doesn't matter. Because I can't marry you ... because we don't even know each other and you're so much older than I am."

"Mona was a good judge of people and she wouldn't have said that if she didn't think we would be a good match."

Then it clicked in Rebecca's mind. She'd

had a conversation with Mona where the woman said she'd find a good man for her, and she'd agreed for Mona to do so. "I only talked with Mona for a couple of hours. I don't see how she could've been a good judge of me at all in that short space of time."

"Sometimes that's all it takes."

Staring into his warm hazel brown eyes, she said, "I can't believe you're actually considering this."

"I'm not only considering it, I am determined to make it happen."

She felt sick to her stomach. "I'm sorry, it's not going to happen."

"Who is going to take care of my *boppli?*" he asked.

"You. He's yours."

"I work."

"Maybe you'll have to leave off work or arrange your work around the *boppli.*"

"It would be easier for me if we married."

Rebecca was horrified. Marriage was for

love, in her opinion. It wasn't for a man to have a free caregiver for his child. "I'm not going to marry for convenience sake. Especially when that convenience is not for me. I work, too." She frowned at him wondering how he could want to pursue what he'd been talking about. "Good day, Jacob." She walked away from him feeling perplexed and, deep down, just a tiny bit cruel. The poor man had lost his wife, but she had to get the idea of marrying her out of his mind. It just wasn't going to happen.

Rebecca had always figured she'd have time to decide whether she would get married or not. She was still eighteen, after all, and none of her friends had gotten married yet. Although, three of them had paired up recently and would probably marry soon. She looked around for Dean and when she saw him talking to his brothers, she walked over.

What Jacob needed was to see her talking

to people her own age and then he would realize she was far too young for him. And if he didn't realize it, she would get her father to have a talk with him.

She hadn't mentioned the bit about what Jacob had promised to Mona because she thought it would be forgotten. The whole incident was way too embarrassing and she didn't know until today exactly how serious Jacob was about his promise. Surely her father would see things in a far different light. She could almost hear him say, *you can't make a promise on somebody else's behalf. Marriage is something that takes two people to agree to become one.* At least, that was what she hoped her father would say.

"Hello, Dean."

Dean smiled at her and then stared at his brothers until they smirked and walked away.

"Hi, Rebecca. I was just coming up to see you."

"Were you?"

"*Jah*, I was. I was going to ask you if you'd come on a buggy ride with me sometime."

"*Jah*, I would. Tonight, after the singing?" She hadn't intended to stay for the singing, but she would if Dean wanted to take her home.

"*Nee*, not tonight. I'm not staying on. I've got to be up early tomorrow."

"I was also thinking of not staying." With a quick look away, Rebecca scanned the crowd for Jacob hoping he'd see her talking with Dean, but he was talking to other people.

"I see you were looking at Jacob over there, and I heard the news."

Her breath caught in her chest. Had Jacob been talking to people and telling them that they were getting married? "What news?"

"Mona died. Your *Dat* announced it during the meeting. She grew up around here."

"Oh, *jah,* that news. I was there at the time when she died."

"Jah, that's what I heard. She died in childbirth."

"Nee, she didn't." The last thing she wanted was for that misconception to circulate around the community. No one would ever use her or Marilyn as a midwife again. "She was fine after the baby was born. She died two days after."

"Oh?"

"Jah. Please don't say what you just said again, and if you hear someone else say it please correct them."

"I will. It must be tough on you."

"It was, it really was. It made me rethink about being a midwife."

"You can't let that stop you, Rebecca. Random things happen all the time and you can't let that sway you. You've wanted to be a midwife from as far back as I can remember. You used to talk about it when we were walking home from school and I'd be embarrassed."

She giggled. "Why embarrassed?"

"Because it is women's kind of talk. You used to tell me way too much detail."

"It's not exactly women's talk. Men make *bopplis* too."

"Stop it, Rebecca, or you'll have me blushing."

The two laughed. He was good company and he supported her decision to be a midwife and that was a plus. After looking over her shoulder at Jacob again, she said, "And when will we go on this buggy ride?"

He looked down at the ground. "Um, can I let you know?"

"Sure, there's no hurry." There kind of was a hurry, but she couldn't let him know about Jacob's promise.

· · ·

ON THE WAY home in the family buggy, she overheard distressing news when her parents discussed Jacob's move to Pleasant Valley. "What's he moving here for?" she asked them.

Her mother turned halfway around. "He wants to be surrounded by Mona's family and friends."

"Who's moving here?" one of the younger brothers asked.

"No one you know," Rebecca answered him. "But doesn't he work?" she asked her mother.

"He's figuring that out," her father said.

Her mother said, "He'll get lots of help from people around here. And he knows that."

Rebecca nibbled on the end of her fingernail. Was he moving there for her? *Jah*, of course, he'll get a lot of help. Where is he moving?"

"Into one of Samuel Kauffman's houses. He's got one that's just come vacant recently."

Should she mention something to her father, so he could put an abrupt stop to the promise Jacob made to Mona? The embarrassment of it all made her decision easy. She would tell no one and pay Jacob no mind and he'd give up his quest.

CHAPTER 4

ON MONDAY, Rebecca headed to Karen's house. Karen rarely went out anywhere these days because it was difficult to go out with the twins, Casey and Caleb, who were just starting to walk. Karen flung the door open with a beaming smile.

"They're asleep."

Rebecca giggled. "Oh, this is your alone time. Do you want me to come back later?"

Karen said. "*Nee,* don't you dare go anywhere. I need someone else to speak with besides Jason and the boys. The boys don't understand what I'm saying most of the time, and I fear it's the same with Jason."

They sat down on the couch and Rebecca's mind was on whether she should tell Karen her troubles or forget them and hope they'd go away.

"That was a joke, Rebecca."

Rebecca looked up. "What was?"

"About the men in this house not understanding me." Karen shook her head. "Don't worry. Tell me what's on your mind. I noticed yesterday at the meeting you looked troubled."

"Okay, I'm going to tell you something that I have never told anybody." She proceeded to tell Karen what had happened— how she'd been alone with Mona and Jacob during Mona's final minutes and about the deathbed promise Mona had forced her husband to make.

Karen pushed herself back into the

couch. "Oh my! I can see why you were so upset."

"I would be upset even if that were the end of it, but he's acting on this promise."

"How do you know?"

"He said something to me yesterday about getting to know one another first."

Karen raised her eyebrows and sighed. "He's in a hard situation."

Rebecca's lips turned down at the corners. "He never should've made a promise like that."

"Let's not think about that now. She said it, he agreed, and here we are now."

"So, what are we gonna do about it?" Rebecca asked the woman who was like a big sister to her.

"Just ignore it. He can't hold you to something like that. Did you also agree at the time?"

"*Nee* I didn't. Um... "

Karen leaned forward. "'Um' what? That was a yes or no question."

"Well, it wasn't the same thing at all. That first day I met with her we were talking about men and she asked me if I'd let her find me a good man and I said yes." Rebecca raised her hands in the air. "Who could refuse an offer like that?"

Karen shook her head. "You're right. It's not the same. Not at all. When you disagreed with him on it, that should've been the end of it."

"*Jah,* Mona wouldn't have thought about it too much when she said it. It was just that she was in a panic. I don't even know how she knew she was going to die. She told him she'd had a dream, but could that really happen?"

"Maybe ... or maybe you know, just before you die, that it's going to happen."

Rebecca groaned. "Anyway, I feel better talking with you."

"Don't worry about anything. He can't force you to marry him and neither can anyone else."

Rebecca put a hand over her fast-beating heart. "You're right. Of course you are."

"It's been a very stressful time for everybody."

"I'm not looking forward to going to the funeral. Do you remember Mona when she lived here?"

"I do; she was older than my friends and I, but I remember her. You would've been too young."

Rebecca nodded.

"And will the viewing be at your *haus?*"

"*Nee,* at Samuel's place as far as I know." Rebecca bit her lip not wanting the viewing to be at her house. "That would make sense anyway."

"I suppose it would, seeing Jacob is staying with Samuel."

CHAPTER 5

BEING THE BISHOP, Rebecca's father had gone early to the funeral and then she and the rest of her family arrived. They couldn't all fit in the same buggy, so Daniel, the third oldest of the bishop's children, had driven one with the next five of their brothers while their mother drove the other.

Rebecca walked into Samuel's house holding Joel and Andrew's hands, her two youngest brothers. Joel was the second youngest at six. Andrew was the 'baby of the family' at four-years-old, 'and a half,' he made sure to tell anyone who asked. In the living room, Rebecca was faced with Marilyn holding the new baby. Rebecca walked over to say hello. "You both stay with me," she told her brothers. "No running off, you hear?"

"*Jah*, Rebecca," they both answered.

"How is he?" Rebecca asked Marilyn as she peered down at the peacefully sleeping baby.

"Just perfect. He hardly ever cries. I think I've only heard him really cry once or twice. He's eating and sleeping just fine."

"See the *boppli*?" she said to her younger brothers.

"*Jah*," Joel said, as Andrew looked around rocking on his feet.

They weren't interested at all. Rebecca noticed Jacob talking to her father and one of the elders. "How is Jacob doing?"

"He's hardly said anything these past days. He's very quiet. Mary said that he was never this quiet. Also, I found out from hospital records that Mona had Eisenmenger's syndrome. She'd been advised not to have children, and I'm guessing that was why she came here to give birth. I'm surprised she survived the birth with the strain it would've put on her heart."

"So, what does that mean? It had something to do with her heart?"

"*Jah*, it's a rare congenital condition, a structural defect that affects the heart and lungs."

"You were right, then. And that was why she came here so late in her pregnancy. Why wouldn't she have had the baby in a hospital?"

"She wouldn't go near them. You saw how she was about getting the paramedics there."

Andrew suddenly broke away and Rebecca had to let go of Joel's hand so she could run to catch her youngest brother. Her father disapproved when his children misbehaved even slightly. He was the bishop after all and his whole family had to be a good example to the rest of the community. It was what was expected of all the oversight families.

Andrew was not old enough to understand that his father was the bishop and that he needed to behave. When Rebecca caught up with him, she went to grab his hand, but he plopped down on the floor and pulled his hand away, tucking both of them under his legs.

"Need some help?"

She looked up and saw Jacob.

"Oh." She gave a little chuckle. "This is my *bruder*, Andrew. The youngest. He's a little bit of a handful sometimes."

Joel ran up to them, and said, "Don't be naughty, Andrew. I'll get in trouble too."

"Boys, this is Mr. Raber. Say hello." When the boys were silent, she said, "This is Andrew and my helper is Joel."

"Hello, Mr. Raber," Joel said.

"Hello, Joel." Jacob then got down to Andrew's level. "Why won't you hold your *schweschder's* hand?"

Andrew shook his head.

"Your *bruder* will hold Rebecca's hand."

"*Jah*, I will," Joel said, taking hold of her left one.

Andrew shook his head again.

"Perhaps I should get *Mamm?*" Rebecca said.

Andrew jumped up, shaking his head emphatically. *"Nee, nee, nee!"* He took hold of her right hand. "Not *Mamm*."

Jacob chuckled. "I think he's putting one over on you, Rebecca."

"*Jah*, most likely. No one is as strict as *Mamm*."

"Maybe you should take a few lessons from her before you get married." He stood up, gave her a small smile and then turned and walked away.

She stood there, bracketed by her little brothers and wondering what he meant by that remark. Was he still expecting to marry her? Did he mean she had to get lessons from her mother before they married, so she could better raise Micah?

Whatever he'd meant, it had been rude to suggest she wasn't good enough. She had raised most of her brothers, well, helped *Mamm* raise them. And she knew what to do. It was just that Andrew was a special case. None of the other boys had been like him. He had an extra amount of energy and stubbornness from somewhere, and he took special handling as a result.

Rebecca's mind was awhirl. She couldn't rest easy until she knew what was going on in Jacob's mind. The sooner he got that ridiculous notion out of his head, the better she would feel.

. . .

AFTER THE VIEWING, everybody followed the funeral buggy to the graveyard. Rebecca chose to stay in the buggy with Andrew who had chosen that moment to fall asleep.

A little later on Rebecca climbed out and stood next to the buggy, looking at the crowd of mourners. It was a shock to everybody that a woman so young had died. There was an extra dollop of sadness that her son would grow up not knowing his mother.

Rebecca couldn't keep her mind from wandering to the upcoming Monday. She had an appointment to accompany Jennifer Byler to a clinic for an ultrasound and she thought again if she'd be better off forgetting about becoming a midwife.

Mona's death preyed on her mind and she wondered if she could've done something to prevent it. Should she have called somebody—or told Marilyn that the woman hadn't looked right—that first night she saw her? Perhaps there was something she could have done and didn't. The burden weighed heavily on her shoulders. Rebecca looked up to see her great aunt heading toward her.

"What are you doing over here by yourself, Rebecca?"

"Andrew's asleep in the buggy."

"He still has his afternoon naps?"

"Not every day. I think it was the movement of the buggy that caused him to fall asleep."

"That's right, it always used to do the same with my Kenny. Your *mudder* told me you were troubled by something."

She knew Agatha hadn't come to talk with her by chance. "It's nothing."

"I hear you'll soon be going on buggy ride with Dean."

Rebecca stared open mouthed at the older lady. "How could you possibly know that?"

She chortled. "I overheard a few people talking."

"Dean?"

Aunt Agatha nodded. "I always thought you and Dean would marry."

"Well, it's a possibility."

"You think so?"

"I don't see why not. We've always gotten along well. We've grown up together."

Aunt Agatha narrowed her eyes. "What's stopping you?"

"Nothing. Things are proceeding okay if you know what I mean. I can't give too much away." She faked a secretive smile and wished something more were going on with Dean. They didn't even have a time arranged for that buggy ride.

"Ah, I see. Your secret is safe with me. I wouldn't want you to wait too long, like Karen did. She was nearly thirty before she got married."

"Um, I think she was twenty-eight."

"*Jah,* and that's nearly thirty."

"She doesn't look like she suffered too

badly over it. She and Jason seem very happy together and now she has twins."

"Just don't waste your time."

"*Denke,* Aunt Agatha, I won't waste any time."

Aunt Agatha gave her a smile and a nod. Rebecca knew she was being a bit offhand with her great aunt, but she didn't want her to launch into the speech about things being easier when you're younger. Every passing year made it more difficult to find a husband in the Amish community. In the meantime, Rebecca didn't want to make an error in judgment. She'd heard too many horror stories from Mary about her first marriage.

When the funeral was over, everyone went back to Samuel's house. Rebecca didn't mix with the adults, preferring to stay with her younger brothers.

CHAPTER 6

WHEN MONDAY ARRIVED, Rebecca headed to Jennifer Byler's house. She was having an ultrasound because she was convinced she was having twins and Rebecca had only been able to hear one heartbeat through her stethoscope. It was just routine, but still, Jennifer had never had one before and didn't know what to expect and that made her nervous. Rebecca had offered to accompany her. She was driving to Jennifer's place in the buggy and from there they were getting a taxi.

Just as she was leaving her house and had

pulled the buggy out onto the road, she saw Dean coming toward her in a wagon. He waved her over and she pulled the buggy off to the side of the road.

Once his wagon was off the opposite side of the road, he jumped out and ran over to her, hat in hand. "I've been meaning to talk to you." In that moment, she admired how handsome and windswept he was. He smoothed back his shoulder-length sandy hair and put his hat back on.

"You have?" she asked.

"*Jah.* I couldn't ask you at the funeral, but I was wondering if you want to go out sometime this week?"

"Sure, when would you like to do that?"

"Wednesday night?"

Her mind ran over the appointments she had on Wednesday. "Late afternoon, when I finish work?"

He grinned. "I can collect you around five if that suits?"

"From the *haus?*"

He nodded.

She couldn't help noticing how blue his eyes were in the morning light, and his skin looked so soft and honey-colored. Everything about him was pleasing. This was the man she would marry and it was about time they set things in order. Her midwifery meant less to her now since Mona had died. "Great, I'll see you on Wednesday."

"Jah. Gut, okay." He flashed a big smile with his perfectly-straight white teeth. She could only imagine how sweet and handsome their children would be.

THE WHOLE TIME at the clinic that day Rebecca was thinking about her date on Wednesday night. Hopefully, things would go well and then she would be officially a couple with Dean. Pressure from Jacob would be off her, too. During the ultrasound, Jennifer was disappointed to learn she wasn't having twins. Rebecca told her that twins were a handful anyway, and one was much easier. That didn't work and Jennifer was still upset, having convinced herself she was having twins. Rebecca didn't have much sympathy because she knew a couple of women who weren't able to conceive at all, but she did her professional best to sound soothing.

ON THE WAY back home from Jennifer's house, Rebecca stopped by Karen's again.

Caleb was crawling around the floor and his twin brother, Casey, was trying to pick up a knot in one of the wooden floorboards. Caleb then pulled himself to his feet with the help of the rough bricks on the stone fireplace, which, thankfully, wasn't lit.

"What if you give Jacob a chance? He's a

lovely man," Karen asked as they sat in the living room keeping an eye on the twins.

"It's kind of too late to give him a chance because now I've agreed to go out with Dean and it's all going to happen."

"What? Careful you don't ..."

"I just want to see how we get along, if we're suited to be more than friends. I'm not going to deliberately jump into a relationship with Dean to get out of one with Jacob."

"That's very sensible."

"Although if it happened, it would save me from that problem." Rebecca put her hand over her mouth and giggled.

"But you don't have a problem. I think it's all in your own mind now. He hasn't mentioned it again you said."

"That's right. He hasn't. But what's going on in his mind?"

Karen raised her hands in the air. "Perhaps, nothing, absolutely nothing. You're just scared and worried over nothing."

"You think so?"

"I know it."

"Thanks for talking to me, Karen. You've always been like a big *schweschder* to me. Like another *mudder*."

"Let's just leave it as a *schweschder*."

"*Jah,* like one of those."

"If you watch these two, I'll make us a hot cup of tea."

"Sure." Rebecca sat on the rug playing with Casey and Caleb. As she watched them, she wondered if she should just marry and stay home with *kinner*. It seemed safer than being a midwife.

Karen was right, Jacob probably would forget all about that promise, given time.

WHEN REBECCA GOT BACK HOME that afternoon, she walked into the kitchen and saw Timothy, her only older *bruder*, sitting there drinking a mug of coffee. He'd been away for two months. She ran to him and hugged him. What she needed was some good older-brother advice.

"Hey, what's all this about?" he said with laughter ringing in his voice.

"I missed you, that's all." She sat next to him.

"I should go away more often, if I'm missed so much. What's been going on?"

It was a rare moment when no one else was in the kitchen. "I have to tell you something that nobody else knows. Well, not many."

His eyebrows arched and he leaned forward. "What is it? Have you been having an argument with one of those girls again?"

"*Nee.*" There were twins in their community, April and May, who always got on the wrong side of her, but it was never her fault. "It's nothing like that."

"You certain? I know May and April said

some pretty nasty things to you, and told a few lies."

"That's in the past. We're friends now, kind of. They stay out of my way and I stay out of theirs.'"

"Good. I'm glad to hear it. Don't look so worried, it can't be that bad. Nothing is ever that bad."

"This is pretty bad for a lot of different reasons." Over the next half hour, she told Timothy how Mona had died, the promise Jacob had made and what Jacob had said to her since. Then, she confessed how she doubted herself now as a midwife. "Well, what do you think about all that?"

He shook his head. "It's a lot to take in."

"I know it's ridiculous to think I should marry him, but that doesn't stop me from feeling guilty."

"Have you told *Dat?*"

"*Nee*, of course not." She shook her head.

"You said you'd told someone."

"Only Karen, I think. *Jah,* only Karen. I can't tell *Dat* something like that. It's too awful."

"You should tell him; especially if this Jacob guy is taking it seriously."

"He was at the start, but I think he stopped now that I let him know I'm not interested."

"See? You're off the hook already. Now, what's the next problem?"

Rebecca sighed. "I doubt myself as a midwife, now. I keep thinking there was some clear sign I should've picked up, but she checked out as normal. She did have an elevated temperature, but she wouldn't allow us to call paramedics. Even the day she died she said no to calling the ambulance."

"You can't blame yourself for things like this."

"I've never attended a birth alone. I've always been with Marilyn until both she and I are confident that I can do it alone. And I don't think I'll ever be confident again, and I don't want to waste any more of Marilyn's time. She's put a lot of time and effort into teaching and training me and everyone thinks I'm going to take over. I just don't think I can do it."

"This is what you've talked about for years. This is what you've always wanted to do."

She hung her head. "I don't know. Everything seems different now. Every time I go to an appointment I keep thinking of Mona."

"You have to find a way to put that out of your mind. You have to be more professional about it. Take what you can and learn from what happened, and move on. Apply that knowledge in the future. If this is what you have chosen to do then do it with all your *Gott*-given ability."

"Do you think so?"

"*Jah,* I know so, so stop being such a young *maidel.*"

"What do you mean?"

"It seems you want to be protected all the time. At some point, you've got to be on your own. You can't rely on our parents or Marilyn forever. You have to become a woman and stand on your own two feet. I left and worked away from the community and feel better for it. Like I was able to truly grow up."

"What if I just got married and stayed home and raised *kinner?*"

"Do that if you want."

"I've always thought I wanted more than that. Bringing babies into the world was such a joy."

"Then you've got to find a way to get that joy back."

She drummed her fingertips on the table. "Under the circumstances it's quite hard. Oh, and I didn't tell you the worst."

"There's more?"

She nodded. "Jacob is moving here, to this community."

"For you?"

She shrugged. "Who knows. He says that he is moving here so Micah can grow up around Mona's family because he doesn't have much nearby family of his own. But what if he's really coming to live here so he can fulfill the promise to his late wife?"

"You want me to talk with him?"

"Nee." She shook her head. "Don't get involved." She felt better not knowing what was on Jacob's mind. If Jacob talked to her brother and the news wasn't good she wouldn't be able to face it.

"Just let me know if you ever want me to and I can talk with him."

"Denke, Timothy. I'm glad you're back."

"Me too. I'm never gonna leave here again. No bed's as comfortable as my own."

Rebecca giggled, thinking he'd been going to say how he missed his brothers or his mother's cooking. She knew she had to continue being a midwife after talking with him. She didn't want to be just an ordinary mother staying at home raising her own *kinner*. She wanted to be out and about helping other women. It was a dream she had always had, so she decided to take up her brother's suggestions and be more professionally minded. She'd have to put what happened in the past and move on.

Their young brothers ran in then, excited to see Timothy, and they dragged him off the kitchen chair.

He said over his shoulder "We'll talk later on the same subject."

"Okay and *denke* again for listening."

He went outside and she remembered she'd forgotten to mention that she was going on a buggy ride with Dean. She hoped that would solve her problems. But she didn't want to jump into a relationship with him just to avoid being in a relationship with

Jacob. Karen could've been right and Jacob might not have given her two more thoughts.

Even though Jacob hadn't mentioned anything lately, Rebecca could scarcely think of anything else. It would've been better for her if he'd moved back to his own community and stayed there.

CHAPTER 7

WEDNESDAY AFTERNOON FINALLY CAME, and Rebecca was teased a little by her younger brothers about going out on the date with Dean. She took the humor in good spirit and didn't let it bother her.

It was an important occasion—the first time she'd gone on a buggy ride with anybody. She'd been asked by a few boys before but had refused them. To her knowledge she was the first girl Dean had asked.

She took her time bathing and then getting dressed and ready for their date. She wanted to look the best she could, and, so she would smell good, she dabbed lavender oil behind her ears. Her tummy fluttered with butterflies when she heard a buggy. She opened the door a little and saw it was Dean.

She called out, "I'm going now. Don't wait up." She closed the door and walked to his buggy.

Just as she stepped into Dean's buggy and they'd greeted one another, she noticed another buggy heading toward the house. She recognized the horse and buggy as Samuel's, but when it drew closer, she saw Jacob in the driver's seat.

As Dean headed down the driveway, Jacob smiled and waved at him and all Rebecca could do was keep her eyes to the front.

Once they got onto the road, Rebecca said, "I wonder why he's at the *haus?*"

"Probably just talking to your *vadder* about his move here."

"You know?"

"Yeah, everybody knows it."

"When did you hear it?"

"At the funeral. Everybody was talking about it. We'll have to make this a quick one tonight. I have an early morning start tomorrow. I have to wake up at four."

"Okay." She was upset. She'd taken so much care to get ready and he had on his old work clothes as though he'd come directly from the fields.

"I've never taken anyone out before," he said smiling.

"This is my first."

"Two firsts." He chuckled. "It must be a sign."

"A sign of what?"

Without thinking he replied, "Compatibility. I always thought we were."

She smiled. "Me too."

He drove around the streets and all they did was talk about nothing important. They didn't even stop anywhere for a bite to eat as she had assumed they would. Rebecca was starving.

When Dean's buggy drew up back at her house, Samuel's horse and buggy were still there. She'd have to speak to Jacob.

"Denke, Dean," she turned to him, wondering if he'd say or do anything romantic. He hadn't so far.

"No problem," was all he said—not even 'you're welcome'—and then he sat holding the reins and waiting for her to get out.

This was not how she'd envisioned her first buggy ride ending. The whole thing from start to finish had been disappointing. As soon as she stepped out of the buggy, he wasted no time in turning it around. She stood and watched him leave. It was still early. *Has he double-booked the evening; is he off to see another girl?* Immediately, she recognized that negative thought and pushed it away. After inhaling deeply, she headed inside.

When she walked into the living room, Jacob was there with his baby in a basket. "Hello, Jacob. I didn't realize you were coming for dinner."

"I was expecting you to be here."

She looked at her mother and father sitting with him having an after-dinner coffee.

"Rebecca is often not home. You never know when she's going to be home and when she's not," her father said peeping over the top of his glasses.

"She's doing an excellent job as midwife, too," Jacob said.

She sat with them, still in her coat and black over bonnet. *"Denke,* that means a lot to hear you say that."

"Jah, of course, you are. Why would you doubt it?" he asked.

"Well, because of what happened."

"No one could've foreseen what happened. It was no one's fault. Mona refused to go to the hospital and she knew she was ill. She knew what she had and kept it from everyone including me. That's the choice she made and you did everything you possibly could have done, and so did everyone."

Rebecca nodded, trying not to think about that day. Mona must've seen her illness as God's will and that was why she didn't seek help. Some folk were like that, but her father didn't support that theory of belief in *Gott*. She looked down at the baby and then, moving from her chair and kneeling down beside him, said, "He's so lovely."

"He's a sweet *boppli*." Jacob looked down at him with pride. "I'll be living a couple of doors from Samuel. The house isn't grand, but I'll buy my own in time once I sell the one in Holmes County."

It sounded too final for Rebecca's liking. "Oh, you're not leaving that as backup?"

"*Nee,* I won't be going back there. I'm changing everything so I can live here ... so we can live here," he corrected himself.

"I've kept dinner hot in the oven for you."

Food. She was starving. *"Denke, Mamm."* She excused herself and headed to the kitchen.

When she was finishing up her meal at the table, Jacob stuck his head through the door. "Good night, Rebecca."

He'd taken her by surprise. She swallowed her mouthful. "Goodbye, Jacob."

CHAPTER 8

WEEKS PASSED and Rebecca couldn't help being curious when she heard Jacob had moved into his new house with a woman. He'd been back to his old community for a bit, and then come back here again. Surely he hadn't married already, but he had seemed kind of rushed when he'd been prepared to marry her right after Mona's death. He could've found someone to marry when he went home.

She couldn't ask her father or mother and wouldn't have to because Mary would know what was going on. Rebecca wasted no time getting herself in front of Mary to ask.

"It's his older *schweschder*, Anne. She never married. I believe they share the same father, but different mothers."

That was too much information for Rebecca to process. But she did feel relieved that he wasn't married and that shocked her a little.

"How are things going with you and Dean?" Mary's face beamed.

"Not as good as I would've hoped. You see, he took me on a buggy ride but since then I found out he also took two other girls on buggy rides. Timothy found out and told me."

"There's nothing wrong with that."

"It's not what I was looking for. I felt like I was settling on Dean and now I feel like Dean thinks I'm not good enough for him, but he doesn't know that I was talking myself into him. I'm so confused." She rubbed her forehead.

"You don't have to be confused at all. You don't have to marry anybody. And certainly not when you're only eighteen or nineteen."

"How old were you when you married?"

"I was older—and all my friends were a bit older. I was twenty-three when I married Damian and that didn't work out so well."

"I know. And that also makes me cautious. I want to make sure I marry the right one."

"I'm sure you will. Don't try to force somebody into an ideal that you have in your head. Just let things happen naturally."

"That's how things worked out with you and Samuel?"

Mary giggled. "Samuel was the last person—the very last person—I saw myself with, but he surprised me. I thought he was one way, from what I'd seen of him, then I found out he was nothing like that."

"I don't get what you mean."

"I thought he was uncaring, unkind, all business and things like that. But he is just the opposite."

"That's interesting that you say that."

"Don't worry so much. Just be happy and go about living your life. As you said, you never were that keen on Dean anyway. You can't choose someone when you're eight and then stick with that decision." Mary laughed at her own words.

"It was ten, but I hear what you're saying. I'm still upset with Dean for casting me aside and going out with those girls. It's offensive."

"It's rare that a man gets married after just going out with one girl. Maybe he was just seeing what they were like before he chose you, making sure he was making the right choice."

"You're not making me feel any better, Mary."

Mary giggled. "Forget about Dean then.

That's my advice. There, does that make you feel better?"

"Somehow, it does." What she couldn't tell her friends was how she was getting curious about Jacob and wanting to know more about him. The only thing was, had she brushed him aside too soon?

REBECCA SLEPT late and walked into the kitchen. Most of the children were at school except for the two youngest, who were playing in the living room.

Her mother turned around from the stove, and said, "I'm feeling under the weather today and I was going to take that casserole I made yesterday and an apple pie over to Jacob and Anne."

"I'll take it," Rebecca said before she could stop herself.

"Will you?"

"*Jah.*"

Her mother gave a weak smile. "*Gut.* I was hoping you would."

REBECCA HELD the basket of goodies with one arm and knocked on the door with her other hand. A woman she guessed must be Anne opened the door.

"Hello, I'm Rebecca, Bishop Elmer's *dochder. Mamm* sent me over with a casserole and a pie."

"Ah, that's lovely. I'm Anne. Come inside. I'll call Jacob and tell him you're here."

Just as Rebecca was breathing in the pleasing aroma of something baking, Jacob appeared at the door behind Anne. "No need to call me. Hello, Rebecca."

"Hi, Jacob."

"Why don't I make us something to eat?" Anne asked.

"*Nee,* I'm fine *denke.*"

"Sit for a while, will you?" Anne asked.

"Sure. I'd like that."

While Anne took the basket into the kitchen, Rebecca followed Jacob to the living room and they both sat down. The house wasn't too small, as Jacob had implied when he'd first told her about it.

"*Mamm* sent some food."

"That's kind of her." Without drawing another breath, he said, "I saw you with some young man the other day when I had dinner with your family."

"*Jah,* we grew up together and our families are close. His name is Dean, and he was taking me on a buggy ride."

He drew his eyebrows together. "Is there anything serious now between you and Dean?"

He seemed jealous and a small part of her was pleased about that. "There could be." She glanced behind her, not wanting to be overheard by Anne. "Look, you and I just were never going to happen." She figured she should be bold and set him straight. She didn't want his expectations to be raised to think that there was any kind of hope between the two of them.

"Are you going to marry him?"

She shrugged her shoulders. "I don't know."

"If you think about marrying him, would you think about marrying me?"

She shook her head. Even though she was intrigued by him, this was too soon. *"Nee."*

"Why not?"

"For one, the age difference is too much."

He leaned back in his chair. "Does age really matter?"

"I think it does. You're nearly the same age as my *vadder.*"

He laughed. *"Nee,* I'm not."

She wasn't so sure about that. Her father just looked older than his age of forty-two because of his gray hair and beard. "So may I ask your age?"

Jah, um ... I suppose you do have a right to know that." He looked down and then brought his eyes back to hers. "I'm thirty-three."

Rebecca raised her eyebrows at that. "Why don't you marry someone closer to your age?"

"I don't think we have any more to say to one another if you have that attitude."

Anne came back in with food and a pot of hot tea. "Now, where do I know your name from, Rebecca? I'm sure Jacob has mentioned you."

"Anne, this is one of Micah's midwives."

"That's right. I heard what a comfort you were to my *bruder* on that dreadful night."

"I tried. It was an unexpected and difficult situation."

Anne nodded and then proceeded to pour the tea. "*Jah,* it was a shock to us all, what happened. Will you stay for some freshly made ginger cake?"

"*Nee denke,* I was just about to leave, but whatever's baking does smell delicious."

"It's just come out of the oven. Do stay! We've had few visitors and I'd like to get to know some people in the community before the next meeting."

"Okay then, I'd love to," Rebecca agreed. "How is Micah?"

"He is a dream of a baby and sleeps nearly all the time."

"That's good."

"Well, I'll leave you two ladies to talk. I have some work to go over with Samuel."

Jacob left them alone and drove off in his buggy. Rebecca was a little annoyed at being left alone with his older sister. She might not have agreed to stay if she had thought it would be just the two of them. "Are you staying on with Jacob?"

"Jah, I am. He needs somebody to look after him and Micah."

"You must be such a comfort to him. Did you also live in Holmes County?"

"That's right. Our parents had only just recently died, and that's why it has hit Jacob extra hard to lose his *fraa* just after. My *mudder* died when I was ten and our *vadder* married again and together they had more *kinner.* Jacob was one of those *kinner.*"

"That must've been hard for you."

"Maryanne was nearly like my own *mudder.* We were close."

"I feel so bad for Jacob. I can't help the way things turned out." Those words just slipped out of Rebecca's mouth.

"Of course you can't. No one can help how things have turned out."

She stared at Anne and guessed she must be around sixty. "Did you marry?"

"Nee, I never did. I took care of our parents and that took all of my time."

Rebecca nodded and felt an affinity with this woman. She had looked after others rather than marry. She reminded Rebecca of Marilyn. "You've got to meet Marilyn on Sunday. I'll bring her to meet you. She's the community's midwife. She never married either."

"I'd like that. I need a circle of friends. Speaking of circles, do you know of a knitting circle?"

"I do. My great Aunt Agatha is in one of those, and she's always looking for new ladies."

A smile spread across Anne's face, making her look years younger.

CHAPTER 9

WHEN REBECCA LEFT Anne after two cups of hot tea and three slices of cake, she passed Mary's house and figured she'd call in and say hello. First, she made sure Jacob's buggy wasn't there. She didn't want him to think she was following him.

Mary ran out to her before she could even get out of the buggy.

"Rebecca! I was just walking outside to call you."

Rebecca stepped down. "What's wrong?" There had been so many bad things happen lately that her mind immediately went to a bad place.

"Nothing's wrong. Everything is right. I just found out this morning and … Samuel and I are expecting our first *boppli* together."

Rebecca squealed and ran to her and the two women hugged. "I'm so happy for you."

"Samuel is beside himself with joy."

"I imagine he would be."

"How did you know to stop by?"

"Oh, I was passing because *Mamm* had some food to take to Jacob and Anne. I thought I'd say hello before I headed home."

"Come inside." As they walked arm in arm toward the house, Mary said, "We're keeping it secret for a few months. It's only early days. I got a test from the pharmacist and took it this morning."

"Your secret's safe with me."

"*Jah,* I know that. You've always kept my other secret."

"Yours and Beth's secret. I told you it's

not my secret to tell. Not even Karen knows. She still doesn't, does she?"

"*Nee.* You wouldn't have known either if you hadn't been a birth helper to that out-of-town midwife that day. How did you come to be there anyway?"

"The midwife was a cousin of Marilyn's and Marilyn asked her to take me under her wing for a couple of months, so I could see how another midwife does things."

"That's right. Marilyn recommended her. I'm just glad Samuel knows the truth about Lois now." The pair sat in the living room.

Rebecca suddenly knew without question that she had to continue in her midwife work.

"Getting pregnant again reminds me of Mona and I know how she would've felt about wanting Micah to have a *Mamm*. That was the sole reason I handed Lois over to Beth and William. I know the ache Mona would've had in her heart. The ache to give her child the best life possible. She saw you as a *gut mudder* to her child. And you'll be a *wunderbaar* parent, Rebecca."

"I would love a *boppli*. Do you really think I'd be a *gut* parent?"

"The best."

"Speaking of Lois, where is she?"

"Freda is teaching her to roll out pastry."

Rebecca sighed. "That woman must be such a blessing."

"I can't tell you how much. I rarely have to cook. I do most of the cleaning, but I've never been a good cook. That was a lot of the problem between me and my late husband, but we won't talk about him today."

"*Nee.* We won't. We'll celebrate the happiness of your news."

Happiness filled to overflowing in Rebecca's heart for her good friend. Mary and Samuel had been trying to have a child for a couple of years and now they were finally expecting.

. . .

AN HOUR later she left Mary's house and, when her house came into view, the last person she expected to see just sitting on the porch was doing exactly that. It was her mother. *Mamm* rarely sat doing nothing, but there she was.

Rebecca left her horse near the barn and headed over to her.

"Okay, Rebecca. I have something to tell you. I heard from Magda that Dean has taken two other girls out for buggy rides. She's not happy with the girls."

Magda was Dean's mother. "I've heard that too. April and May."

"Not them!"

"*Jah.*" Rebecca nodded. They were the worst two people in the world he could've chosen. Rebecca had never gotten along with the twins. April was the older, born just before midnight on the very last day of April, and half an hour later, her sister was born on May first. Their mother thought it cute to call them April and May, but Rebecca knew there was nothing cute about those two. *"Jah, it's so, Mamm."* Rebecca sighed. Now she could never marry Dean. He'd betrayed her and embarrassed her in front of her mother and anyone else who knew she'd gone on a buggy ride with him.

"I'm sorry, Rebecca. I can't see how he took both of them out."

"One after the other, or both at the same time?" Rebecca asked.

Hannah giggled. "I'm hoping it was one by one."

"Who cares? Not me, not anymore." Rebecca guessed it would've caused a rift between the twins.

"Here's a buggy now. Is that Dean?"

Rebecca looked over. *"Jah,* it is."

"Here's your chance to speak with him." Her mother left her standing on the porch.

She leaned on the railing and watched him pull up his horse and walk toward her.

"Aren't you going to say hello?" he asked.

She looked him up and down, and said a curt, "Hello."

He pushed his hat back slightly, grimaced, and planted his feet wide apart. "I guess you heard about May and April?"

She scrunched her shoulders, and walked up to her horse and buggy. "Nothing to do with me. I need to unhitch my buggy." She proceeded to do just that, ignoring him.

"Look, Rebecca, can you stop that for a moment?"

"*Nee,* the horse needs to be rubbed down. I don't know how you treat your horse, but my *vadder* taught me how to look after horses properly, and if a job's worth doing, it's worth doing well."

He hung around until she was finished and her horse was in his paddock. "Can we talk now?"

She dusted off her hands. "Okay. Well, you can talk because I have nothing to say."

He looked down at the ground and rolled a tiny pebble around underneath the sole of his shoe. "I didn't want you to be the only woman I'd ever taken on a buggy ride."

"Well I'm not now, am I?" she said through gritted teeth, annoyed with herself that she'd as good as agreed to marry him when she was ten years old.

He took hold of her hand, pulled her into the barn and closed the door behind them. *"Nee.* I didn't come here for you to give me a hard time, Rebecca."

She scrunched her nose. "What did you come here for?"

"I came here to ask you to marry me."

She gasped. "What?"

He flashed her a perfect smile with his white straight teeth. "Rebecca Shroder, will you marry me?"

She put her hand over her heart and took

a moment. Out of all the girls, he could've asked, he was asking her. She was flattered, and everything about him was right. His looks, his family … but, could she forgive the April, May thing? "Are you sure?" she asked.

"I've always been sure about you, Rebecca."

"I don't know what to say."

"Just say *jah.*"

She wondered if he'd kissed April, or May, or both. He'd cut the buggy ride short with her, and had almost seemed bored with her. What if April and May weren't so boring to him. "Um … I'll have to think about it."

He drew his eyebrows together. "What is it you have to think about?"

"My feelings were hurt when I heard you took those other girls out. You had to know that those very two girls are not friends of mine, and in the past, we've had fallings out."

"Just childhood quarrels. Anyway, would

you have preferred me to take out your good friends?"

"My good friends would have refused you because they would have known ..."

He shook his head. "I can't take back what has been done. I'm sorry I have disappointed you already before our marriage has even begun."

"It's just that it was an unfortunate choice for you to make."

He smiled again, his confidence returning. "Well, let that be the last unfortunate choice I ever make. Would that make you happy?"

"I guess so. *Jah.*"

"Denke." He quickly drew her into her arms, planted a kiss on her lips before she could stop him, and yelled, "You won't be disappointed." He hollered and threw his hat into the air so high it nearly reached the wooden rafters.

"Wait, I didn't agree to that."

Her father flung the barn door open and adjusted his glasses. "What's all this commotion? Why are you two alone in here together?"

"Bishop Elmer, your *dochder* has just agreed to marry me."

A look of delight spread across her father's face. "I knew it. It was just a matter of time. I was saying that to Hannah only today." He jumped forward and kissed Rebecca on her cheek, and then shook Dean's hand, and then patted him on his back.

Rebecca felt sick to her stomach and didn't know what to do. Things only got worse when her mother joined in the congratulating. She would tell them later that it was all a misunderstanding—a silly miscommunication—and she looked over at Dean who was smiling. Had he got things wrong or had he deliberately jumped to that conclusion because he couldn't stand to be rejected?

"She wasn't sure and then she agreed. I'm the happiest man in the world."

Timothy, munching on an apple, walked out of the house, and asked, "What's going on?"

"Rebecca is getting married," their father said.

"Who to?" Timothy took a bite of the apple.

"Me, of course," Dean said.

Timothy looked at Dean in surprise and then looked at Rebecca. "Is that right, Rebecca?"

His question was drowned out as their mother and father dragged the young couple into the house.

Then, her father, his hand on Dean's shoulder, took him to the next room to have a private word. Rebecca looked out the window at Timothy who was still standing there, stunned. She felt exactly the same.

CHAPTER 10

WHEN REBECCA WENT to bed that night, she realized she'd already let things go too long. She should've spoken up sooner. Now they even had a wedding date and her mother, who'd forgotten how upset she'd been over Dean showing interest in April and May, was highly excited at the first of her *kinner* getting married.

It was all a huge mistake and first thing in the morning she would go to Dean's place to tell him the engagement, the one that she'd never agreed to, was off.

Rebecca couldn't sleep and when she heard noises in the kitchen, she poked her head in hoping it was Timothy, and it was. She needed to speak with someone and he was the only one who hadn't been pleased at the news she was marrying Dean. "Can't sleep?" she asked.

"*Nee,* I'm in shock." He held his head in his hands.

Amused, she asked, "About Dean?"

"*Jah.* I told you already what I think of him."

She thought she'd string him along a little. "You don't think we'd be good together?"

"I don't think he's got the right motivations."

What else had Dean done? Or, was he only talking about April and May? "In what way?"

"It's like this Rebecca; you are the bishop's *dochder* and I think he's the type of man that thinks it looks good for him."

"What does? To be marrying the bishop's *dochder?*"

"*Jah.*"

"That makes me feel dreadful."

"Don't take it the wrong way. He could love you. Everybody should, in my opinion because I know all your good points, but does he even know you? Does he know you at all?"

She remembered back to their extremely short buggy ride. "Not that well, I guess. Only from when we were young. Anyway, it was all a big misunderstanding. I didn't even agree to marry him."

"So, you're not going to marry him?"

She shook her head. "*Nee,* I'm not. Here's what happened. He asked me to marry him and I said I needed to think about it. Then I said *jah* to a different question and then he thought I was saying *jah* to marrying him. Then he yelled, *Mamm* and *Dat* got involved, and the whole thing spiraled out of control. It was really awful and I didn't know what to say. I felt like it was happening to someone else or something. Everyone was just so excited and I was in shock. You saw the looks on their faces?"

"I did. You've got to say something—and do it quick."

"I know I do. I'm not going to marry him just because of a misunderstanding."

Timothy threw his head back and laughed. "Rebecca, you do keep me entertained. Only you could get yourself into a situation like this."

"That's nothing to laugh about. How do I get myself out of this situation now?"

"Just be honest and tell everybody the truth. Right away."

She crinkled her nose. "The truth makes me look like an idiot."

"You're not an idiot."

"I feel like one most of the time. I'm always getting myself into bad situations."

"Oh, you mean like the situation with the other fellow—Jacob?"

"Exactly. I visited Anne and Jacob yesterday."

Timothy blew out a deep breath, and leaned back in his chair. "Why would you go and do a thing like that? I thought you would've kept well away."

"*Mamm* had me take a pie to them and a meal."

"The man's crazy for you, so do you think that was wise? Let me repeat myself. The man's crazy for you."

"*Nee,* he's not crazy for me. It's nothing to do with me. I could've been anybody in that room that day."

"But it wasn't anybody, Rebecca, it was you. You have to stop getting yourself into these scrapes."

She took a deep breath. "I'll try."

"The first thing you have to do is tell

Mamm and *Dat* what you've told me now. I'll go with you."

"Will you?"

He nodded. "After you."

"What, you mean right now?"

"Right now. Let's go."

Rebecca woke their parents and they weren't too happy about it.

To hush their protests, Timothy said, *"Mamm, Dat,* it's important you hear what Rebecca has to say." Timothy folded his arms and Rebecca sat on the end of their bed. "When I told Dean *jah,* I didn't really agree to marry him."

Her mother frowned. "What are you saying, Rebecca?"

"He asked me to marry him, and I said I needed to think about it, and then he asked me something else as well. I answered yes to the other question. I never said I'd marry him."

Shaking her head, her mother seemed to

doubt her words. "Then why would he think you agreed?"

"I'm not sure. Because that's what he wanted to hear?"

Her father said, "Why keep quiet when we were arranging a date for the wedding?"

"Everyone was so happy and excited, and I think I was kind of in shock. I didn't know what to do."

Her mother said, "Oh, Rebecca, you've made a mess of things. Tomorrow I was going to talk with Dean's *mudder* to arrange the sewing of the wedding suits and dresses. I know you'd be too busy to sew with your work."

Rebecca slumped her shoulders. It was odd her mother would be upset about May and April and then think it was fine to suddenly marry the man who'd disappointed her. "I'm sorry. I'll tell Dean tomorrow and apologize to his parents."

"And there's more," Timothy said leaning against the doorpost.

Fear ran through Rebecca and she stared at Timothy. *"Nee,* that's all."

"There's the Jacob thing."

Rebecca frowned at him, shaking her head. She hadn't meant that she was going to tell her parents about that too.

"What 'Jacob thing' is this?" her father asked.

"It's nothing. Nothing at all."

"Rebecca?" her mother asked in a no-nonsense voice while Timothy, realizing his error, was slowing edging out of the room.

"Stay put, Timothy," their father said. Timothy froze and cast his eyes downward. "What is 'the Jacob thing,' Timothy?"

"Nothing."

Rebecca was trapped. She had to say something, and all she could think of was to tell the whole truth. She told them what Mona had made her husband promise.

"Oh, the poor woman," her mother said, regarding Mona, while the bishop shook his head.

Were they also going to blame this on her? Rebecca wondered. "I had nothing to do with it. I was just there at the time."

"Has Jacob discussed this matter with you?"

"*Jah.*"

"And?" her mother asked, nearly leaping out of bed.

"I told him it couldn't happen."

"Then he should leave you well alone," her father said.

"*Jah,* he is."

"*Gut.* I'm glad you told us. Don't ever be afraid to tell us anything, Rebecca."

Rebecca jumped to her feet. "I feel a whole lot better now that you know."

"But, you could've told us in the morning," their father said pointing to the battery powered clock on the nightstand. It was three thirty.

"Sorry, *Dat, Mamm*. It was my idea," Timothy said.

Timothy and Rebecca left their parents alone and headed back to the kitchen. "*Denke* for throwing me to the wolves in there."

Timothy chuckled. "I thought you were going to tell them."

"*Nee*. I'd only intended to tell them about Dean."

"It worked out okay, didn't it?"

Rebecca nodded. "I guess it did. It was hard at the time, but now I'm glad they know. The pressure is off me."

CHAPTER 11

THE NEXT MORNING, Timothy had left by the time Rebecca woke up, and there was a note in the kitchen for her from him. She sat down while her mother made her some breakfast. The note asked Rebecca to meet him in town at twelve at a coffee shop they used to frequent.

"Where's Timothy gone, *Mamm?*"

"He didn't say. He just said be sure that you got that note. Now, I think we should talk about Dean."

"*Nee*, please, *Mamm.* I can't … I don't want to talk about him."

"You've made up your mind?"

"I wasn't even given the chance to think about it. Let's just say it's on hold. I'll tell him today."

"You'd better do it soon."

"I'll do it when he finishes work." She was not looking forward to that conversation.

LATER THAT DAY, when Rebecca arrived at the coffee shop as arranged, Timothy was nowhere in sight. But Jacob was there, sitting at a table by himself. It was too much of a coincidence. Timothy had to have arranged this. That was confirmed when Jacob looked up at her and waved her over.

She moved forward and sat down in front of him. "What's this about, Jacob?"

"Timothy called me this morning and told me everything from your viewpoint."

Inwardly, she grimaced. What had Timothy said? Had he told Jacob about the mix-up with Dean and his marriage proposal? If so, she'd feel a real fool. "What did he say?" she looked around. "Is Timothy coming? He asked me to meet him here."

"He's not coming. He wanted you and me to talk alone."

"Oh."

He continued, "He wanted us to clear the air about the madness that I thought I should marry you because of my *fraa's* request."

"There's no need to apologize. I'm sure you thought you were doing the right thing."

He nodded and looked down. "She must've been delirious to make me make a promise like that." He looked up at her. "Can you ever forgive me?"

With Dean, everything was just ordinary. Now, there was a different feeling with Jacob. As much as she wanted Dean to find her special, she wanted Jacob to look at her like that even more so. "There's nothing to forgive. You were just doing what any good husband would do. You were thinking of your family and that's only normal under the circumstances. Under the very unusual circumstances."

"I'm glad you're so understanding."

"I'm learning to be more so as I get older." She gave a little giggle.

"That's right, I forget sometimes how young you are. You're far too young to think about marrying someone like me. It's just that you seem so much older than your years." He looked away again. "Your *bruder* told me you're only eighteen."

"Nearly nineteen." She stared into his unusual hazel brown eyes, noticing flecks of gold and green.

"I'm sure Mona thought you were older. You were so skilled as her midwife."

She snapped back to reality when he mentioned Mona again.

"I guess you can be free of any obligation I might have made you feel, and you can marry Dean now."

She knew from his words he didn't know about the awful thing with Dean that happened the previous day. As she stared at the swirls in the abstract painting behind Jacob, she was glad all the way down to her toes that Timothy hadn't told him about the Dean fiasco. It was a weird feeling to have thought she'd marry Dean for most of her life and now he was a disappointment.

Just as she opened her mouth to speak her mind, something she used to be well-known for, he said, "No one could replace her."

And there was her answer. It was madness to marry a widower who would always be comparing her to his first wife. She stood up. "I should go."

"Can I walk you out?" He jumped to his feet.

"Of course."

"Friends?" he asked.

"Always."

He gave a low chuckle when they walked out the door of the coffee shop. "I feel I've embarrassed myself."

"Anyone might've done what you did under the circumstances."

"I doubt it, but I'm glad you said so."

"There's my buggy," she said, gesturing across the road.

He extended his hand and she had no choice but to shake it. When his large hand wrapped gently around hers it sent tingles through every fiber of her body. She wondered if he felt it too. Without looking at him, she pulled her hand away from his and hurried to the safety of her buggy.

As she drove away, she glanced in her rearview mirror to see him staring after her.

That led her to wonder if he felt something for her in some small way. Now she knew she needed a man like him and not a boy like Dean. Dean had the body of a man, but he was still a boy inside. What she needed, and wanted, was a mature man, one who would make her feel secure, who would be able to support her being a midwife. One with eyes for only her.

Now that the pressure was off, she found herself attracted to Jacob's goodness and his kind heart and gentle soul. No wonder Mona had offered him to her; he was exactly the type of man she and Mona had discussed that first night they'd met. As much as Mona had wanted a wife for Jacob, and a mother for her child, the woman had been doing her a huge favor. She realized that now.

CHAPTER 12

KNOWING Samuel would be at work somewhere checking on his businesses, Rebecca
went to Mary's house for some advice.

Once Rebecca was sitting across from
Mary, she leaned over close and whispered,
"I think I really like Jacob."

Mary's freckle-smattered nose wrinkled
with delight. "That's great news."

"*Nee*, it's not. It's all messed up because of
what's happened. And besides, he'd always be
comparing me to Mona. And she sounds like
a pretty incredible person. How would I live

up to that?" She shook her head. *"Nee,* it would never work."

"What if you just take your time and get to know him? I'll have a dinner on Saturday night and invite you both."

Rebecca wondered whether that was a good idea. "Wouldn't that be like a bit of a setup?"

"You're right. I'll invite other people too."

"Like who?"

"I'll invite Karen and Jason."

"Good idea. I would feel much more relaxed with them here and then I can just get to know him with no pressure on either of us. That's great."

"I think he's a good match for you, but …"

Rebecca leaned forward, eager for some older-woman advice.

Mary continued, "It might be a little too early after Mona's death for him to be thinking about someone else. I think he should wait at least a good six months. What do you think?"

"I really don't know. I haven't had any experience in these things. He's just so manly. Nothing like Dean."

Mary's eyebrows rose. "What happened with Dean?"

"He's just too changeable. He finally asked me to marry him."

"And you said no?"

"Of course I did." She didn't embarrass herself by telling Mary the full story of Dean, and the mixed-up question-and-answer business, and even having a wedding date set. "He took other girls out for buggy rides."

"But that was before you were officially a couple."

"We never were officially a couple. There was one quick buggy ride and then nothing. And, the ride was pretty ordinary. He should've known he loved me and only me. I didn't like it that he took those other girls out."

"I think it sounds more like you don't like his choice of girls."

"You know about April and May?"

She nodded. "It's hard to keep anything secret around here."

"We've managed to keep our secret about Lois."

"Shh." Mary looked around.

Rebecca leaned forward. "She wouldn't know what we mean by that. She wouldn't know what secret we're talking about."

Mary said, "We'll have to tell Lois one day when she grows up and I still don't know how that's going to go over. Everybody still think she's Beth child. I don't want Lois to think Beth's her *mudder* when I am. But, I still want her to know that Beth was an important person in her life. I want her to feel Beth was her other *mudder*, if you know what I mean. Just not her main one."

"At least Samuel knows the truth, that's the main thing."

"*Jah,* but how will the community react to the lies we've been living all this time?"

"Maybe she doesn't have to know any different. Just don't mention Beth as anything other than Samuel's *schweschder.*"

"I've thought of that, but what if other people in the community refer to Beth as her real *mudder?*"

"That will probably never happen."

"Maybe you're right." Mary sighed. "If we tell the bishop and the community members right now, Lois will never have to suffer from being confused."

"That sounds like a *gut* idea." Rebecca nodded. "*Jah,* that's probably best. It seems you'll have to face it and confess the truth sooner or later."

"I don't know if I'm ready to face all that drama of all the different opinions that will be flying around."

"If you do it soon, that stuff will all blow over, and Lois will never have to go through life thinking she's someone else's *dochder*."

"You make a good point, Rebecca. I'll talk about it with Samuel tonight."

Knowing how it felt to have the burden of a secret lifted, Rebecca said, "Then tell *Dat*. Talk it over with him and he'll know the best way to handle things."

Mary nodded. "Anyway, you came here to talk about your problems, not mine." Mary giggled. "Why is it that everyone has problems?"

"That's life I guess. With life comes problems. I think it would be wonderful to be married because there would be no more facing problems alone."

Mary smiled a knowing smile. "*Jah*, marriage is good like that."

"You must've noticed a big difference between your two husbands?"

"There's no comparison. I lived in a

nightmare with Damian. A dreadful nightmare. I never knew what mood he'd be in
when he came home."

"Don't even think about it. I'm sorry I
brought it up."

REBECCA LEFT there thinking about Jacob.
She could hardly get him out of her mind.
Why was it that, now that he wasn't interested in her, he instantly became more attractive?

Maybe it was too soon for him to marry
again, but what if she delayed telling him her
feelings and then she was too late? What if
he found somebody else? Then a feeling of
dread ran through her. What if Jacob started
to like April or May?

NOW IT WAS TIME. Rebecca had to tell Dean
that she no longer wanted to marry him, had

never even said she'd marry him, and that he had been mistaken—or presumptuous—in thinking so.

She waited down the road from his house for his wagon to come past. She was too embarrassed to wait at the house and talk to his folks. Dean would've told them she'd accepted his proposal and she wanted to tell him away from them. He could tell them it wasn't happening after she'd spoken to him.

When she saw his wagon making its way toward her she wanted to run. Immediately she felt sick to her stomach. She had to get it in his head she wasn't going to marry him.

He smiled at her as he approached and she wished he didn't look quite so handsome with the wind swirling his hair around his masculine tanned jawline. He put his hand up and waved, and she waved back before she stepped out of the buggy.

He stopped his wagon in front of her buggy. "What are you doing here?"

She held her stomach. "Yesterday, I didn't agree to marry you. I said yes answering you about something else and then *Dat* came in and you told him we were getting married."

"What are you saying? We have a date set and I've told everyone."

"Who have you told? You'll have to un-tell them."

"Rebecca, you don't want to marry me?"

"I thought you were going to let me think about it. That's what I told you yesterday." She had to let him down gently.

"In my mind, there's nothing to think about. Either you will marry me or you won't. Is there someone else?"

"*Nee!* There's not."

He eyed her sceptically and she had to look away from his clear blue eyes.

"How long do you want to think about it?"

"I'm not sure. Not too long."

He groaned. "I don't know. Should it be

this complicated? I must say that this has taken the joy out of it for me. Maybe I should think about it, too."

She opened her mouth in shock. He was taking back his proposal? That bothered her and she wondered ... if it upset her, did she still have feelings for him? "Okay."

"*Nee*. We should forget the whole thing." He turned on his heel.

"Well, if you hadn't taken April and M ..."

He turned back around and now his expression wasn't happy. "I made no promises to you until I asked you to marry me. Before that I reckon I could've done anything I wanted, and asked anyone out."

"You didn't even dress nicely for our buggy ride. You made no attempt. I think you were still wearing your work garb."

"I had no time to change. I had to help *Dat* at the last minute with a fence so the goats wouldn't get out. I thought you'd think less of me if I was late." He looked down. "It seems no matter what I do, you find fault. I can't live with a nagging woman. Goodbye, Rebecca." He turned and walked away and this time she let him.

She got back in her buggy and waited until he was well down the road before she moved her horse forward. It hadn't gone as well as she'd hoped, but at least she'd told him. And it had been his decision to call it all off. Half of her felt like crying over a lost childhood dream, the other half like laughing with relief.

CHAPTER 13

REBECCA HAD BECOME SO nervous about the dinner Mary was having for her sake—so she could get to know Jacob better—that she'd asked Mary if she could bring Timothy along. He'd put his foot in it once before but, on the whole, he was a pretty good brother. Mary had agreed to having an extra guest.

As they traveled together in the buggy, Timothy asked, "What's the purpose of this dinner?"

"It's just a general get together. Jacob's sister, Anne, will be there."

"I haven't met her yet. What's she like?"

"Way too old for you. You really haven't met her yet?"

"Nee. How old is too old?"

Rebecca giggled. "She's about sixty, I'm guessing."

His eyebrows nearly reached his hat and then he laughed. "I agree. That is a bit too old. I'm prepared to go older, but maybe not by that degree. I thought you were going to say she was twenty-five."

"Nee, it's his older half-sister. I guess that's where the age gap comes into it. One of the parents was different. There was a second marriage in there somewhere. I've been told by Anne, but I can't recall."

"You must remember. What if the subject comes up tonight in conversation?"

"Hmm, you're right, let me think. That's right. Okay, Anne's mother died and then their father married again and the second *fraa* had more *kinner* and Jacob was one of them."

"See? You just have to stop and think about things. So, this *schweschder* is helping Jacob with the *boppli?*"

"That's right." She stared at Timothy, determined to give him a taste of his own medicine. "Now, what is Jacob's *schweschder's* name, and the name of his *boppli?* You've got to get all the names right so you don't embarrass me,"

Timothy laughed. "Me embarrass you?"

"*Jah.*"

"I'll never embarrass you. Have I ever?"

"*Jah,* when you forced me to tell *Mamm* and *Dat* about Jacob. And a second time when you arranged that meeting with me and Jacob. That was one of the most embarrassing times of my life."

He glanced over at her. "It worked though, didn't it? You sorted things?"

"I guess so. Watch the road. You never take enough care when you're driving."

"Stop picking on me."

"I'm not—well, maybe I am—but you have to have eyes everywhere when you're driving."

He chuckled. "I don't pick on you and tell you you've been talking to yourself a lot lately."

"When have I?"

"When you've been doing chores."

She covered her mouth with her hand. "Oh, that's not good. That's a habit I'll have to break."

Timothy laughed again. "*Nee,* I'm just kidding."

Rebecca leaned over and thumped her brother hard on his shoulder. "That's not even funny."

He shook his head. "Ah, Rebecca, you'd believe anything."

"Why shouldn't I believe everything?"

"Because that makes you gullible."

"Just for that I'll have Mary seat you next to Anne and you'll have to find something in common to talk about."

"Don't you dare. I wouldn't know what to say. I'd prefer to be seated next to Jason and Samuel. I prefer to sit next to men. I know what to say to them. I've got nothing in common with a sixty-year-old woman, one who's not my *mudder*. And *Mamm* is younger than that."

Rebecca shook her head. "That's not how these dinners work. Men and women sit alternating, one by one."

He shook his head. "I don't know why I agreed to this."

"*Jah*, you do. A good meal cooked by Freda."

"That's right, it was a tempting offer, but I can't help thinking that you're up to something." He stared at her, momentarily taking his eyes off the road and placing the reins in one hand.

"The only thing I'm 'up to' was that I didn't want to go to this dinner alone."

"Because of the whole awkward Jacob thing?"

She shrugged. "Of course. That's right. I just want everything to be normal again."

"Fair enough."

When they pulled up at Mary and Samuel's house, Luke was there to take care of the horse. At first, Timothy was reluctant to let the horse go.

"Luke knows what he's doing, Timothy. Come on into the *haus* or we'll be late."

Timothy stared at Luke and then handed over the reins. "Look after him please, Luke."

Luke smiled at him. "I know what to do, Timothy."

Timothy and Rebecca walked toward the house. "Try not to embarrass me."

"How would I?" Timothy asked.

"Just try to fit in. Samuel and Mary lead a bit of a posh lifestyle. They have money."

"And how would I embarrass you?"

"Just go along with things, like Luke taking the horse."

He sighed. "Gotcha."

"Just agree with everything and go along with everything."

"Good."

Rebecca added, "And don't ask what the food is if it's something unusual. Just eat it."

"Hey, who gave you permission to boss me around? You're younger than me."

Rebecca poked him in the ribs. "Just do what I say."

They stopped talking when Mary opened the door and greeted them with Lois holding onto a handful of her dress. They exchanged hellos and Mary then showed them into the living room where everyone else was waiting.

"Oh, we're the last ones to arrive?" Timothy asked.

"*Jah,* this is all of us," Samuel said.

Rebecca saw the baby basket and walked across the room. She hovered above the basket, admiring the sleeping baby for a moment before she sat down. When they were all seated, Mary excused herself to see how far away the dinner was. Rebecca looked around awkwardly, wondering how to start the conversation. She also noticed that Karen and Jason weren't there.

To her shock, Timothy began, "And you are Jacob's *schweschder?*"

"*Jah,* that's right. I'm Anne."

"I'm Rebecca's older *bruder,* Timothy."

"Oh, I'm sorry. You two haven't met each other before," Rebecca said.

"It's my fault," Jacob said. "I should've made the introductions. I don't know where my mind is tonight."

"How are you enjoying Pleasant Valley?" Timothy asked Anne.

"I've been here before not long ago."

Rebecca knew she meant she had come for Mona's funeral.

"And how are you enjoying living here now?" Timothy asked Jacob.

"Hard to say. I've not been here long enough."

Timothy nodded and then there was more awkward silence. It didn't appear Jacob was trying to be very friendly.

"We've been looking at houses," Jacob said then, "but there don't seem to be too many coming onto the market."

"It's a slow time of year," Samuel said.

At that moment, Mary came back into the room. "The dining room is ready."

They sat down to a table full of roast chicken and other roast meats, fresh and cooked vegetables, mashed potatoes and a variety of salads. Rebecca glanced over at Timothy and saw him looking at the food strangely. She was glad she'd cautioned him to keep quiet.

"This all looks lovely, Mary," Anne said.

"*Denke,* but it's all Freda. I didn't do much at all."

"You wrote the menu," Samuel told her with a smile.

Mary giggled. "I guess I did that."

Timothy looked around. "Where is Lois?"

"She's eating in the kitchen with Freda."

When Micah cried, Jacob went to stand, and then Anne said, "*Nee,* you stay. I'll get him."

When Anne was out of the room, Samuel cleared his throat and looked at Jacob. "It must be a blessing to have Anne here with you."

"*Jah,* it is. It's a blessing she was able to move here."

"It's a big move to leave everything and come here, Jacob," Timothy said. "What made you decide to make the move since you haven't grown up here?"

"It's for Micah. He won't have his *mudder,* so I wanted him to have all her relatives around him."

"That was very considerate."

"Karen and Jason weren't able to come?" Rebecca asked Mary.

"*Nee,* they were coming, but then the twins weren't too well. Just something going around, nothing serious."

Rebecca was sure that the conversation would've flowed more easily if Karen and Jason were there with their twins livening up the room and distracting everyone. Or maybe the twins would've been in the kitchen with Freda, too.

Jacob said, "Are Karen and Jason friends of yours, Rebecca?"

"Karen is a good friend of mine and Jason's my cousin, and they have one-year-old twins."

Jacob nodded. "I know who we're talking about now. Karen works part-time for us in the lumberyard." He looked over at Samuel.

Samuel said, "That's right. She only works two and a half days now, since the twins have come along. I don't know if you know this Rebecca and Timothy, but Jacob is a partner in a couple of my businesses and one of them is the lumberyard."

"*Nee,* we didn't know that," Timothy said.

Samuel smiled. "Jacob and I have known each other for many, many years."

At that point, Rebecca knew that if she wanted to know anything more about Jacob she could ask Mary. In turn, Mary could find out from Samuel—in a very subtle way, of course.

Just when they were about to begin dessert, Anne came back into the room. "I gave him a little of his bottle and now he's back to sleep."

"He's such a dream of a *boppli,*" Mary said.

"Lois was just like that. She's still a good sleeper. She still has a nap in the afternoon."

Anne nodded as she started eating her food.

"He mostly sleeps and eats," Jacob added.

"I can heat that up for you, Anne. It must be cold by now."

Anne shook her head. "It doesn't bother me. Rebecca, don't forget to introduce me to your aunt from the knitting circle."

"Great Aunt Agatha?" Timothy asked looking at Rebecca.

"Jah, that's the one. Anne wants to join a knitting circle and Aunt Agatha is very involved."

"Our Aunt Agatha is involved in most things," Timothy told Anne.

Anne gave a sharp nod of her head. *"Gut.* I should get to know her."

CHAPTER 14

HALFWAY THROUGH THE DESSERT, a help-yourself feast of cheesecake, fruit salad, chocolate cake, and ice-cream, Rebecca felt someone looking at her and she looked up to see Anne staring at her. Had she caught her looking at Jacob more often than she should have been? Did Jacob's sister know what was on her mind?

After the coffee and after-dinner mints, Rebecca noticed Anne yawning and decided it was time to go. She gave Timothy a nod and then he stood and said they would call it a night.

"So, how did that go?" Timothy asked as soon as their buggy left Samuel and Mary's property.

"What do you mean?" Rebecca asked.

"Did I embarrass you there?"

"Only a little, but not much." She shot him a smile. "You did well."

He gave a little grunt. "You didn't make it half obvious."

"What's that?"

"You kept staring at Jacob."

She gasped. "Did I?" Now she knew that was why Anne had been staring at her. "I didn't mean to."

"But you were."

"That's why Anne kept looking at me strangely."

He stared at her while the horse clip-clopped down the darkened road. "What's going on?"

"Don't look at me, look at the road."

"Trigger knows his way home."

"All the same, keep your eyes on the road."

Timothy looked back at the dark, tree-lined winding road shaking his head all the while. "I just hope you know what you're doing."

"I don't know what you're talking about."

"Well, you seem to have changed a lot since we talked a few days ago."

"Since then Jacob has apologized to me and said he didn't know what he was thinking. And that was during the meeting you so kindly arranged—without my permission I might add."

"He's using reverse psychology on you."

"What? What did you say? Reverse … what?"

"Psychology. When he sees that chasing you isn't working, he pretends he's not interested. And it's working for him."

"Don't be ridiculous."

"That's making you interested, isn't it?"

"I'm not."

"I can tell you're interested in him now. I needn't have given him my older *bruder* speech. I should've left things the way they were."

"Stop talking, Timothy."

"I just had to know what you were doing. You're young, he's old and then there's the *boppli* to take on. The *boppli* who's not yours."

"Don't you think I know that?"

"And then if you do get married, what will happen to the old *schweschder*?"

"Her name's Anne."

Timothy shrugged. "Picture the future if you marry Jacob. Anne's left her life behind in … wherever they came from. She can't go back now. She'll be living with you forever, constantly telling you what to do and looking over your shoulder. It'd be like living with *Mamm* forever. You'd never feel like it was your home. Who would Jacob listen to if there was a disagreement? His new, much-younger *fraa,* or his older *schweschder,* who'd given up all to live with him and the *boppli* in their hour of need?"

She bit the inside of her mouth. She hadn't thought of all that. "Don't talk."

"Okay. I'll be quiet."

WHEN REBECCA SLIPPED between the sheets that night, she wondered if she hadn't been too dismissive of Dean. Girls mature faster, and Dean had a lot of growing up to do. In five years, he'd be more mature and a different version of himself. Timothy had a good point, there were a lot of barriers now in marrying Jacob, but no such barriers existed with Dean. Dean's life was a clean slate compared to Jacob's.

Besides, if she married Dean or someone

young like him, she'd have the say-so as the woman in the household, and there'd be no first wife to be worried about being compared to. She now knew why everyone said that marrying young was the best way.

CHAPTER 15

THE NEXT DAY was Sunday and Rebecca was looking forward to seeing Jacob again. Mary was the first person she saw when she walked into the Millers' house where the meeting was being hosted. She and Lois were sitting in one of the middle rows.

"Can I sit here?" she asked Mary.

"*Jah,* of course."

She took her place on the wooden church bench. It wasn't very comfortable, but there she would sit for the next hour and a half for the meeting. "*Denke* for dinner last night. It was the nicest meal I've had for so long, and even Timothy said so."

Mary smiled. "I'm glad you came, and I'll be sure to tell Freda." Mary looked around. "She's here somewhere."

Rebecca looked around as well, but she wasn't looking for Freda.

"He's not here yet," Mary said.

Rebecca stared at Mary's smiling face. "Who?"

Mary leaned in. "I'm not talking about Dean."

Rebecca shrugged.

The next people to come into the room were May and April. They sat directly in front of Rebecca but two rows up. They didn't even look at her, but smiled and said hello to Mary.

Rebecca didn't say anything, but wondered why they seemed upset with her. There was something about those two girls. She wanted to like them, but she just couldn't. And then next into the house came Anne with the baby in a carrying basket. She sat in the first unoccupied seat. Jacob came five minutes after and sat in the front row on the men's side.

Then Rebecca saw May digging April in the ribs and they both looked at Jacob. May leaned toward April and whispered something. Rebecca desperately wanted to know what they were saying and she might have been able to hear them if she had been sitting one row behind instead of two. *Is it possible one of them likes him?* They were her age, so it seemed odd for them to like someone so much older. Did they know she liked him, and were they deliberately trying to get under her skin? That would be just the sort of thing they would do.

Throughout the meeting, Rebecca couldn't concentrate on what her father preached in his sermon, and she generally liked listening to him. The whole time she was staring at Jacob and found he did everything in a manner that suited her. During the sermon, some men would murmur their agreement or say 'amen' in a loud voice. Jacob did none of those things. All he did was sit, listen attentively and look up the scriptures in his bible.

After the meeting, she stayed in the house and introduced her Aunt Agatha to Anne. The two of them seemed to hit it off immediately. After that, she moved outside to where the food was being served and saw both May and April speaking with Jacob. She moved just close enough to hear what they said without appearing to be eavesdropping.

May said, "So, any time you want help with Micah, just call us. Or if you want housework, sewing or anything done."

"*Denke*, that's very generous," he said. "Perhaps it's best to talk with Anne. She arranges those things."

"We already talked to her just now," said April.

"Jah, and she said to speak with you," May continued on with her sister's lie.

Rebecca knew it was a lie because she'd spoken to Anne immediately after the meeting was over and May and April hadn't been anywhere about, and Anne and Aunt Agatha were still talking together.

He scratched the side of his head. "That is unusual. I'll have to speak with her, but we're handling things okay on our own. Maybe that's why Anne said to speak with me—because we don't need anything."

May said, "Neither of us work and we'd like to help out if we can."

April added, "How about we come over tomorrow?"

"I do ... I will be doing work from home soon, but I'm in and out all the time. I can't say if I'll be at home, but Anne might."

"We'll stop by tomorrow and take our chances," May said.

"Yeah, we'll see how we can help. There must be something we can do."

"*Denke*, that's very nice of you."

May and April then left him alone and he looked in Rebecca's direction and caught her eye. She smiled at him and he walked over to her.

"Everyone is so friendly around here," he said.

"Some of them are, that's for sure and for certain," Rebecca said. "It was good Anne could move here with you."

"I am blessed with a good *familye*."

He smiled at her and all the while Timothy's words rang through her head. She'd never be the top woman in his life. Not with his sister about. When someone else came up to speak with Jacob, she moved away.

She decided to drown her sorrows in

food. When she was piling food onto her plate, May and April came alongside her.

"How well do you know Jacob?" May asked.

"Hello, to both of you."

"Yeah, hello," April said. "May just asked a question."

"I know him a little bit. Just the same as I know any newcomer."

"Did you deliver his *boppli?*"

"I did. Along with Marilyn."

"Then you were there when his *fraa* died?" May asked.

"She didn't die in childbirth." She thought she'd point that out firmly. Those were the rumors circulating. "She died a couple of nights later, and, yes, I was there at the time. She had a heart problem that no one knew about. Why do you ask?"

"That must be so sad for him." April shook her head appearing sad. Although, Rebecca doubted that either May or April was capable of genuine emotions.

"Was he really in love with her?" May asked.

"Of course he was." *What are they up to?* From her past experience with these two, they were trying to trip her up into saying something dreadful and then they'd tell everyone what she'd said. She had to be careful.

"I heard that she was a lot older," April said, lowering her voice.

"Was she? I never really noticed. I couldn't really say," Rebecca said and then turned back to the food table.

"We've heard some things and we thought we'd ask you."

Rebecca swung around to face May. "What?" She narrowed her eyes at them. "What have you heard?" Had they heard about Jacob's promise to his wife? Only a few trusted people knew that information. Unless someone else at the house that night had overheard Mona. Her parents and Timothy and her good friend certainly would've kept it to themselves.

"Do we tell her, April?"

April shrugged her shoulders. "Might as well."

May said, "There's a rumor going on that there's something between the two of you."

"That's absolutely ridiculous. Like what?"

"We're not sure yet. But we will find out," April said leaning forward and staring into her face.

Rebecca leaned back at them. "The man's lost his *fraa*. Don't start thinking of some drama or lies that will hurt everyone involved. I won't hesitate to tell my *vadder* if you do."

"Maybe we'll have something to tell Bishop Elmer before you do." May looked at April. "Let's go."

Rebecca shook her head and was glad

they were gone. The twin sisters had been trouble since she'd met them when they were all five years old, and nothing had changed. They always tried to upset the people around them. Rebecca heard giggling and looked over to see May and April laughing at something between themselves.

When Rebecca had filled her plate, she sat down to eat. Just as she had eaten her first mouthful, she saw May and April had gone over to fuss over the baby. The baby was in the basket between Anne and Jacob. She kept watching and then noticed Jacob was talking with them again. If she moved over there and listened, it would look too obvious. Looking around for someone she could send over, she spotted Timothy. He looked up and caught her eye and she waved him over.

He sat down. "What's up?"

She looked over at the two girls speaking with Jacob. "Don't turn around now but behind you is Jacob. May and April have sat down with him. I need you to go join them and see what they're saying. Then tell me."

Timothy shook his head. "Anything involving those two always ends up making trouble."

"And that's exactly what I'm trying to avoid, trust me."

"Is all of this about the crush you have on Jacob?"

"*Nee*, I'm worried he'll get hurt somehow. You know what they're like. Now go quick. They could be talking about me."

He shook his head and grabbed her plate of food. "I'll need this as a prop." He stood and said, "And because I'm too lazy to get my own food."

When he was halfway over to Jacob, Rebecca headed back to the food table to fill another plate.

. . .

A LITTLE LATER, Timothy headed back to Rebecca.

"What happened?" Rebecca asked when he sat down.

He shook his head. "It was embarrassing. They were throwing themselves at him."

"Are you serious?"

He leaned back. "I'm not joking. I couldn't see them because I had my back to them. I was sitting at the next table, but I could certainly hear what they said. They were trying to get an invite for dinner and asked to help with Micah."

"I meant for you to sit with them and get in on the conversation."

"Nah, I thought it better to listen and observe."

"This is the second time today they've asked him if they could help."

Timothy glanced over his shoulder at Jacob, and then looked back at his sister. "What do they find so attractive about him?"

She looked at Jacob now talking to one of the other men. "He's a real man."

"I thought one of them liked Dean."

"I think they both did."

"Any chance they know that you like Jacob now?"

She shook her head. "I don't think so."

"It just doesn't make sense for them to like a man that age. Or for you to like him, and don't deny it because I know you do. I just need to know how a man like him can attract women."

"Hey, this is about me, not you. You worried you'll be single forever?" she asked Timothy, only half joking.

Timothy smiled and shook his head. "I'm hardly ready for anything like that. I couldn't disappoint all the women in the community by choosing just one."

"I can see what a problem that would be for them."

He nodded. "A huge problem."

CHAPTER 16

THE NEXT FEW days were business as usual for Rebecca and Marilyn.

On Wednesday afternoon, Rebecca learned from her mother that there was to be an emergency meeting at their *haus* that evening, at seven, with the church elders and with Jacob. Her mother was keeping quiet as to what it was about. She always knew everything, but that didn't mean she would tell Rebecca.

That evening, it was Rebecca's job to help her mother by getting all the younger siblings fed, bathed and into their rooms well before seven. Despite the resistance and grumblings of the older ones saying it was far too early, Rebecca managed to complete the task at a quarter to seven.

The meeting of the elders would be held in the living room and the children couldn't be witness to what was said. Many such a meeting was held before someone was shunned, or worse, excommunicated.

As Rebecca put the last of the children in their rooms and closed the doors, the elders were already gathered in the living room and she found herself stuck at the top of the stairs. She couldn't walk down to go to her bedroom because she'd interrupt the meeting; she had no choice but to be still and stay out of sight. She carefully sat on the hallway floor with her back against the wall. Jacob arrived and then she was surprised to hear April's voice. Her voice was similar to her twin's but much shriller.

What April said next was most distressing. She accused Jacob of trying to be inappropriate with her when she went to his house alone on Tuesday morning.

When Jacob's turn came, he had a differing story. "It's not true. I told her I had a meeting and I couldn't stay and chat. I was already running behind time. I didn't even know she was going to be there. Nothing happened. I'm surprised to hear all this now. Anne can tell you. I went into the barn, hitched the buggy and continued to my meeting. April then went in and told my sister something like what she told you. Anne didn't believe it and I'm surprised that I'm sitting here and my good name is being called into question."

She heard the familiar sound of her father clearing his throat. "An accusation has been laid and we are hearing both sides."

"Nothing happened," he repeated. "She talked to me for a moment while I was buckling some leathers for the harness and that was it. I barely even looked at her. I had my mind on the meeting."

When Rebecca heard April's sobs, she rolled her eyes. *That girl! She can turn tears on and off like a tap.* She'd been on the receiving end of April's lies many a time and had gotten into trouble for the lies told by both April and her twin sister.

One of the elders spoke, "We've got someone saying something happened and someone denying it. Would the truth lie in the middle?"

"Absolutely not," Jacob said. "She was talking with me while I hitched the buggy. I barely answered her, and then I left. I was slightly annoyed that she came when she did. I wasn't expecting her and neither was my *schweschder*. On Sunday, she mentioned that she and May might call over the next day, meaning Monday, but they didn't."

"I was just trying to help," April said.

"Why can't you tell them what happened between us, Jacob? You said we'd marry and all would be okay. Now you're saying we won't marry. What we did was a sin. Unless," she sobbed dramatically, "unless we marry now."

Jacob said, "Why are you telling lies before *Gott* and the elders? Nothing happened and I said nothing to you like what you're saying. I barely spoke to you."

"Why are you going back on your word?" she shot back at him.

"It's clear that one of you is not telling us what happened," the bishop said.

"You can ask my bishop if I've ever been involved in anything like this."

Bishop Elmer said, "We will be."

"I have a good name. Has April ever before accused anybody of something they didn't do?"

Rebecca was pleased he asked exactly that, because May and April had made up stories in the past. Surely that would work in Jacob's favor.

"We can't discuss that with you," one of the elders said.

"I'm not asking you to discuss it with me," Jacob said, "I'm merely asking you to take everything into consideration."

"I think the best thing we can do is meet back here Friday night at the same time. Why don't you both go away and search your hearts? We'll reconvene on Friday night and then we'll make a decision on what is to be done."

"I urge you to tell the truth," one of the elders said. "The ramifications of this will be enormous."

Rebecca heard shuffling. "Are we finished now?" Jacob asked.

"We are," Bishop Elmer said.

"Goodbye." She heard footsteps. Jacob was walking to the door. Then she heard the door open and close.

She felt so badly for Jacob. First, his wife dying, and he was suddenly grieving and trying to raise a child alone, and then he'd moved to a new community ... only to have this happen. She knew for a fact that April was lying, but she couldn't prove it. April was trying to force the oversight's hand into telling Jacob to marry her.

"Why won't anyone believe me?" April cried again.

Then Rebecca heard her mother's voice and realized that she'd been sitting in on the meeting. "The truth will come out, April. Don't trouble yourself now. I'll find Rebecca and she could make us all a cup of tea."

"Rebecca's home?"

"She is."

"I should go now. Don't worry about the tea, Mrs. Schroder."

"Are you sure? I don't know if you should be driving yourself in the buggy if you're so upset."

"I'm fine."

"Why didn't your parents come with you, April?" Rebecca heard her father ask.

"Because they don't know about this. I couldn't tell them. I was too embarrassed to talk about it. I thought I'd be believed and now I regret telling anybody what happened. I should've kept quiet and let him get away with it."

Then Rebecca heard the door open and shut. All went silent until she heard the voice of one of the elders. "What do you think, Elmer?"

"I fear this isn't the first time April's made up stories," her father said.

"You don't believe her?"

"I'm keeping an open mind, but that history must be considered, and I'll also contact Bishop Warwick from Holmes County. I already have talked to him about Jacob, and he said he's a man of excellent character. Nevertheless, I'll talk with him again."

"What we probably need is character witnesses on both sides," one of the men said.

That gave Rebecca an idea and she didn't listen to the rest of what was said. If she could get May to tell the truth, everyone would know April had made it all up. She decided to visit May the very next day. First, though, she'd need a good plan. What would it take for May to speak out against her twin?

CHAPTER 17

WHEN REBECCA WENT to May and April's house, she was pleased to find May alone pinning out the washing.

"Rebecca? I'm surprised to see you here. Are you by yourself?"

"*Jah.*"

"You've never visited me before. I'll get April and tell her you're here."

"*Nee.* Don't." She hurried closer. "Have you heard what April's done?"

May nodded. "I've heard rumors that she's made accusations."

"Jah, I heard that too."

"I told her to keep quiet about it."

"Do you believe Jacob would do that, or is she lying?"

May pressed her lips together.

"I know you're not like April. I know in the past she's dragged you into things. One of the men has a clever plan to prove Jacob's innocence and the truth will be found out." Rebecca shook her head. "April is going to look awfully silly and, since you're her twin, people will think of you the same way. They'll assume you both came up with the idea."

"Jah, they do that. Whenever she does something I always get half of the blame."

"Where is April now?"

"She's sewing."

Rebecca glanced back at the house; she had a limited amount of time to speak with May alone. "I'll be quick. If you know a certain person is lying, come to my *haus* at seven on Friday night. The truth's going to come out. I was thinking, what if you were the person who told everyone she was lying? Then a certain man might be very grateful."

She saw May swallow hard. "You mean Jacob would be grateful?"

"*Jah,* think of it. He just moved to a new community and his name and reputation are very important. He would trust you and be grateful to you."

"Only thing is, April would be very cranky with me, and she is my—"

"You know what everyone says about you?"

"What?"

"You follow April around like a puppy dog, hanging on her every word. Everyone sees that she's the leader and you're just the follower."

Her mouth turned down at the corners. "Who says that?"

Rebecca shrugged his shoulders. "Everyone. It's the general thing everyone thinks."

"That's not true, I'm more than just the follower."

"Really? It doesn't seem that way. She is the one who's made up the story about Jacob, so where does that leave you? She's going to be shown to be a liar on Friday. Do you want to be dragged down with her? And if that doesn't happen, you know what will?"

"What?"

"Come on, don't you know why she's doing this? If the elders think some act has happened between the two of them, they'll be told they have to marry."

"Nee!" May's mouth fell open in shock.

"Jah. Didn't April tell you that was her plan? People are told they have to marry if they go too far. It happens all the time."

May scowled. "She knew I liked him."

"The only chance you'll have with Jacob is to tell the truth."

"She didn't even like him until I did. How could she do this?"

"Well, I think there's only one thing you can do about it. You'll have to choose between the man you love and the *schweschder* who is trying to betray you and marry a man under false claims." Rebecca was going to stop there, but when she saw May was hanging on her every word, she continued, "You know, the two of them will have to marry quickly. Everyone will know why the quick marriage, but no one will say anything. It'll all be swept under the rug. You'll be left with no April, and no Jacob. They'll live happily, once Jacob forgives her for what she's done and where will that leave you? It's your choice."

"*Denke* for being such a good friend, Rebecca."

At that moment, April rushed out of the house. "Hello, Rebecca."

"Hi, April. I was just leaving."

"So fast? Why did you stop by if you're leaving so quickly?"

"I was just having a quick talk with May. Bye." She left quickly and as she drove away in the buggy, she heard raised voices. She hadn't meant to make them quarrel, but neither could she think up a good excuse for why she'd been talking alone with May.

REBECCA WAS in her bedroom on Friday night when everyone gathered downstairs for the meeting. She saw that both of the twins were there and she hoped—*nee,* she prayed—for a good outcome.

The meeting was over within ten minutes, and out of her window she saw April leaving in tears. Her mother knocked on the wall of the kitchen, the one that was also the adjoining wall for her bedroom. Rebecca knew that meant her mother wanted help preparing the teas and coffees for everyone. She wasted no time joining her in the kitchen.

"What happened?" Rebecca whispered to her mother.

"April was making it all up. May told everyone that April had cooked up the scheme."

"That's awful. What was her purpose?"

"May said that Jacob truly had paid April no mind and either she wanted to pay him back for slighting her, or she wanted the oversight to say they should marry. And they might've if they'd believed what April said. Now, less chatter and more helping me with the teas and coffees."

Rebecca was delighted that her plan had worked. She'd saved Jacob from embarrassment. Who knew what would've happened if she hadn't spoken to May?

CHAPTER 18

IT WAS the second Sunday of the month and there was no meeting that day. Since Rebecca couldn't get Jacob out of her mind, she thought she'd pay him a visit.

She pulled up in her buggy and he walked out of his house to meet her.

"I'm glad you're here because I need to talk with you, Rebecca."

She got out of the buggy wondering why he wasn't smiling. "Sure. What about?"

He shook his head. "May told me that you tricked her into exposing April."

He knew what she'd done and he wasn't happy, that much was clear. "Tricked her? I just made her see it was best to say so if she knew April was lying." Rebecca didn't see that as something so bad. "Aren't you pleased? You're no longer under suspicion."

"I don't need you doing things like that on my behalf. You told her I'd be interested in her if she saved me."

"Um." She thought back to what she'd said to May, and it was true. She'd made her believe that. "Aren't you pleased? I mean, you're in the clear now."

"I've got no time for childish games. I realize you're just a teenager. And I made the mistake once of thinking of you as a woman. I guess it was because of your vocation that I thought of you as older than you are."

"I can't change my age and I'm sorry if I did something to upset you."

He shook his head and spoke softer. "I just don't have time for games, Rebecca."

"But it wasn't a game."

He crossed his arms over his chest. "It may not seem so to you, but that's what I would call it."

She knew she'd lost him. If he still had held any spark of interest in her as a woman, it was gone. "I was only trying to help."

"I don't need help that comes with deception."

"But it wasn't really deception."

"You led her to believe I'd be interested in her if she got me 'off the hook,' as you put it."

"I'm sorry, I was just desperate to help you. And I couldn't think of any other way."

"I'm a believer that the truth always comes out."

"Only if someone does something. Isn't faith rewarded by works? I mean, faith without works is dead, right? I was just using a little action to help with the faith."

He sighed. "I think you're twisting things to suit yourself."

"I guess we'll have to agree to disagree. And I'm sorry you think less of me now." She walked away before he could see the tears in her eyes

"Wait, Rebecca."

She hurried into her buggy, and slapped the reins on her horse's rump so he took off at a spritely pace, and she did nothing to slow him down despite Jacob calling after her again. What she didn't need was any more of his criticism.

WHEN REBECCA GOT HOME, she hurried into the house and closed herself in her room hoping nobody had heard her come home. She flung herself on her bed. Love was proving difficult. Jacob was a hard man to please, and then there was the age difference. Then again, he might've been more light-hearted if his wife hadn't died. But if Mona had been still alive then she wouldn't be thinking of Jacob at all. There'd only be Dean.

Mona's promise had made everything so awkward. In a few years, Jacob and she might have fallen in love with each other if left to themselves. April and May would never speak to her again, but she wasn't so much worried about them. In fact, she could see that as a blessing of sorts.

OVER DINNER THE NEXT NIGHT, her father told her that April was moving to a small Amish community just outside Ohio and May was staying on in Pleasant Valley. Rebecca kept silent, but she hoped her father would forewarn the bishop of that community. Drama always followed April wherever she went.

As she washed up side-by-side with her mother, the conversation turned to the recent drama with April and Jacob.

"I think Jacob will be glad April's moving. Fancy concocting a story like that." Hannah shook her head.

"It was good that May came forward with the truth. Unfortunately, it seems that has split them. It's a shame really. I mean, they were always together. The truth would've come out anyway," Rebecca said because that was what Jacob had said.

"Well, we were praying that it would. There wasn't a word of truth in what April said. She must be troubled. According to May, she was also instrumental in devising this scheme and she apologized to everyone for it."

"Really? I didn't know that, but it was good of her to admit it."

Hannah passed Rebecca a wet plate. "I think Jacob's fitting in nicely to the community. It's just a shame that there was this upset."

"Are the ladies making Anne welcome?"

"As much as they possibly can, but she's busy with the newborn. I'm surprised you haven't been around there more often, the way you love *bopplis*."

Rebecca placed the dry plate on the stack next to her and lifted them up onto the cupboard shelf. "It's a bit difficult, under the circumstances."

"Ah that?"

Rebecca nodded, glad once again that she'd told her mother about the promise Mona had made her husband make.

"That's all forgotten about, isn't it?" Hannah asked.

Rebecca shrugged. "Can anything like that ever be forgotten?"

"*Jah,* I think it can."

"The whole thing is just awkward."

"Only if you make it so. I think you should talk with him."

"I don't know how I can do that. If I go to his place Anne will be listening in and she knows nothing of it, as far as I'm aware. I don't think it's something that Jacob has gone around telling people."

"Why don't I invite them for dinner tomorrow night? I'll arrange it so you two can have a quiet word."

Rebecca shook her head. "We've already talked about that and more. I don't think he wants to talk with me. Anyway, that would be too contrived. I'll wait until I catch him alone, maybe before or after a meeting sometime and I'll just make sure that we're all good."

Her mother smiled. "That's the way."

Rebecca was pleased her mother was being so helpful with the whole situation.

Hannah's face turned sour when they heard running footsteps from above them. "I have told them so many times not to run in the *haus*."

"I'll go up."

"*Nee*, you finish this off and I'll go up."

Her mother dried her hands on a tea towel and stomped out of the kitchen.

When she was gone, Timothy walked into the kitchen from the back door. "What's up?"

"Ah, just in time." She tossed him a tea towel.

"*Nee;* it was the wrong timing. But I rarely get a chance to talk to you these days and I saw *Mamm* hurrying off. So, what's going on?"

"Well, April's moved away as you probably heard and, I haven't told anybody this, but Jacob thinks I'm childish. He accused me of forcing May to tell the truth about April."

"How can you force somebody tell the truth?"

"I might have led her to believe that Jacob would be very grateful, if you know what I mean."

"Ah, now I get the picture. And he didn't

appreciate you manipulating someone to tell the truth?"

She washed a plate and passed it to him to dry. "I guess you could put it like that, but I thought he'd be pleased the truth was out."

"Ah, men." He shook his head. "We're such strange creatures."

"You've got that right."

Timothy laughed. "I have a different opinion. If a girl did what you did for me, I would be very grateful that she took the time and trouble."

"Well, he wasn't and now I don't think he's talking to me." Rebecca exhaled deeply.

"And you're upset?"

"I guess so."

He moved closer to her, and asked, "What happened to him being far too old for you?"

"Just dry the plates, would you?"

"What do they say about women? 'It's a woman's privilege to change her mind?'"

"I've never heard that."

"They also say 'all is fair in love and war.'"

Rebecca laughed. "You're just making things up."

"I'd never do that. My name's not April."

"You better be quiet. You won't want *Dat* to hear you say things like that."

"Saying what?"

Rebecca and Timothy turned around and looked at their mother in the doorway. She had her hands on her hips looking like she was ready for trouble.

"I was just saying how much I liked drying dishes," Timothy said.

Hannah stepped closer with her eyes fixed on her oldest son. "Is that right?" She walked right up to him and stared him in the face and he nodded. "Well, it's the first of the month, and you can do all the dishes for the entire month."

His jaw dropped. "Are you serious?"

She nodded. "I am. Both the washing and the drying, since you like it so much." Then their mother turned to Rebecca. "Come on, Rebecca. Timothy's got this under control. You and I can sit in the living room. And then, Timothy, I think we'd like a pot of hot tea." Hannah turned and walked out of the room.

Rebecca could barely keep the smile from her face when she saw the look of dread on Timothy's face. She left the dishwashing sponge in the dishwater and dried her hands. When their eyes met, she gave a little shrug. "Sorry," she whispered, and then hurried to catch up with her mother. *All is fair in love and getting out of the dishwashing job.*

CHAPTER 19

THE NEXT DAY, when Rebecca was heading away from the house to a client appointment with Marilyn, Dean flagged her down.

"What is it?" She didn't bother moving off the road. The road had such little traffic on it and most of it was slow moving buggies or wagons. Besides, she didn't think they'd be talking for long since she still had nothing to say to him.

"I just wanted to say I know I've been horrible and a disappointment to you, but I've learned my lesson."

"That's good. I'm glad."

She collected the reins, and he said, *"Nee,* stop. Can you give me a minute?"

Rebecca huffed. "I can give you a minute, but that's literally all."

"Can you not see that I have done nothing wrong? You're acting like I'm the most awful person in the world."

"Am I? You don't think you've done anything wrong?"

"Nee, I don't. What do you think I've done?"

She couldn't say the words. How could she tell him that she wanted to be special and now she felt she wasn't? But, to be the mature person she wanted to be, she thought she would speak her mind even if it sounded silly and might make her feel silly too. "What I wanted was to feel special. I wanted to be the only girl you ever went out with. That's how it was with my folks. And I've always wanted things to be like that. And then you took May and then April for buggy rides. I felt awful."

He looked at her from under his dark lashes, a slight smile on his lips. "I haven't asked either of them to marry me."

"Forget it."

"What you have to say is very important to me. Pull off the road, would you? I'll only take two more minutes of your time."

She was early for her appointment, so she agreed and steered the horse off the road and jumped down and waited for him.

"I won't keep you long. I'll have to say this fast. You are special to me. I want to marry you and I've always wanted to marry you. I'm sorry I thought you said yes to my proposal last time. I didn't mean to embarrass you with your family. I always assumed that we would marry."

She nodded, knowing in her heart he had

always felt the same as she. Timothy's words came to mind. Did he want to marry her because she was the bishop's daughter? "Why do you want to marry me?"

He frowned and screwed up his face. "That's a hard question."

"You must be able to answer it."

"It's a hard thing to put into words. It's because you're you. Everything about you is what I like. The way you glide when you walk, the way your face tightens when you're angry or you disapprove of what somebody's saying. The way you laugh, and can make me laugh. And besides that, our families are close. It makes sense for us to marry. I have feelings for you. Don't you have any feelings for me?"

She stared at his handsome face. She did have some kind of feelings for him, but she didn't know if they were the right ones. "I feel everything is ruined now. You had to know I don't get along with May and April. It upsets me that you even considered them."

"I can't do anything about that now. Anyway, April's moving. The word tells us to forgive."

Rebecca shook her head. "I can't make any rapid decision."

"I did want to get married before the year is out."

Was he saying he wanted to marry just anyone before the year was out? "And what will you do if I say no?"

"If you don't want to marry me I guess I'll have to find somebody who does."

"Oh?"

"Don't look so offended."

"I'm looking offended because I really am."

Dean rubbed his forehead.

"I must go or I'll be late."

"Wait. If you turn me down am I supposed to pine after you for the rest of my days? That's just foolish."

"I'm just trying to gauge what feelings you have for me; it's kind of hard for me since you've gone from me to April to May and then back to me."

"It was May, then April."

"Whatever." She huffed again, not happy about the fact that he even remembered the order.

"What you're looking for is romance and love, I feel, and that's not practical."

"I'm not looking for romance, but I am looking for real love. I want somebody who loves me and I love them in return."

"If you don't marry me, Rebecca, who will you marry?"

She shrugged her shoulders. "I better go now, or I'll be late."

"Where are you going?"

"Work. I've got an appointment to see a lady with Marilyn."

"Rebecca, I think you are the most interesting and fascinating woman in this whole community and I think I might even love you."

She looked into his clear blue eyes and was flattered. But was that good enough? If she said no, he'd just said he'd move on to the next woman. There had to be more to love than that.

Her mind then drifted to Mona. She might have thought there wasn't much more to marriage when she made her husband promise to marry her. It seemed as though she'd also thought one woman was as good as another.

Had Mona just wanted a woman to raise her child with no thought for her husband loving somebody? Was that a reflection of Mona and Jacob's marriage? She recalled how they'd spoken to each other in those final days of Mona's life. She stared into the distance wondering if Mona and Jacob had been very much in love. That was something she didn't know and the only person in the community who might know was Aunt Agatha.

She made the decision right there and then to stop by Aunt Agatha's house on the way home from her appointment. Aunt Agatha knew everybody's business and, since Mona had come from this community … they might even have been in the same knitting circle.

"Why are you staring into the distance like that, Rebecca? Are you rethinking my proposal?"

She looked back at Dean. If she'd been thinking about Jacob in that moment, she knew she didn't have real feelings for Dean. "Dean, I must decline your offer."

"What? You can't be serious. Aren't you going to at least think it over?"

"I am serious, and if you'll excuse me, I must go now so I won't be late."

He called after her. "I've given up a lot for you."

She glanced at him in the rear-view mirror and saw the shrinking figure shaking his head. It seemed nobody had ever rejected him, which was no surprise to her, considering he was so handsome.

CHAPTER 20

WHEN REBECCA ARRIVED at the appointment with Marilyn, she found out the woman, Becky, was a cousin to Mona.

"It was a terrible thing that happened to Mona. That won't happen to me, will it?" Becky asked Marilyn

"It's highly unlikely. That was the first death I've had in fifty years of doing this," Marilyn said.

"And she had a pre-existing condition that she kept secret and wouldn't seek medical attention for," Rebecca added, hoping that would make the woman feel better.

"Oh, that's a relief. I couldn't believe it when I heard about it."

"Were you close with Mona?"

"Not really. All I know is she and her husband were married for years with no *kinner*. He keeps to himself now, he does. He won't even come to our place for dinner."

"It would be hard with the new *boppli* and everything and his *schweschder* with him, and trying to settle into a new home and a new community," Rebecca said.

Marilyn added, "I'm sure once he settles down things will be different."

"I guess you're right."

Marilyn took the woman's blood pressure and then felt around her stomach. "Everything seems fine. How have you been feeling?"

"I'm queasy around cooking smells."

"That's only to be expected."

"And I'm so tired all the time."

"All those things are part of what we women have to put up with during pregnancy," Marilyn said.

"I'm just scared about the birth. Considering what happened to Mona."

"That's made everybody a bit nervous. Everybody we have seen lately is upset about what happened to Mona. But as we said, it won't happen to you," Rebecca told her.

Becky asked them to stay on for lunch and they both declined. The woman was a talker, but Rebecca had found out nothing interesting about the marriage and was even more anxious to speak to Aunt Agatha.

As Rebecca drew up to Aunt Agatha's house, she wondered what excuse she could have for visiting. She would just use the excuse she was passing by after an appointment and thought she would call in and say hello.

She knocked on Agatha's door, and Agatha opened it and then looked past her.

"*Mamm's* not here; I'm here alone."

"Oh. It's lovely to see you, Rebecca. How's the family?"

"Fine, just fine."

"Come in."

"*Denke*. I was just passing after visiting a newly pregnant woman and I thought I'd pop in and say hello. I haven't seen you much lately."

"I've been around," Agatha said.

"I know, but I haven't talked to you much."

"I'm very pleased to have a young visitor. People don't visit as much as they use to: nowadays it seems everyone is too busy."

"Is that right?"

"*Jah.*" She picked up a cat, sat down and placed the cat on her lap. Another cat jumped off the couch. "Have a seat."

"I see you've still got your cats?"

"*Jah*, and I have two more out back. They were unwanted kittens people gave me. I couldn't see them thrown in the river in a bag weighed down by rocks."

Rebecca winced. "*Nee*, of course not."

"Well, that's what would've happened to them if I didn't rescue them."

"Well, I'm glad you did."

"What's happening in your life, Rebecca?"

"It seems that our pregnant women are worried that they'll meet the same fate as Mona, but she didn't die in childbirth or as a result of it. It was a factor of course but only because of what she already had wrong with her heart."

"I can understand that they would be scared. Especially, first time mothers."

Rebecca nodded. "Did you know Mona when she lived here?"

"I did. You would've remembered her, wouldn't you?"

"*Nee*, I was too young, I think. The lady I

was just visiting said they were married for years before they got pregnant."

"That's right."

"How did they meet?"

Aunt Agatha stroked her cat and looked up at the ceiling. "He came here to one of our weddings and she fell instantly in love, and the next thing I knew she was off, moving to his community without a by-your-leave."

"Is that right? And why didn't he move here?"

"I can't say. I don't know all the details, but I always thought they were a strange pair."

"You mean Mona and Jacob?"

"*Jah,* and I suppose I shouldn't say that."

"Why were they a strange pair? You think they were strange with each other? Did she chase him and he wasn't too keen?"

When Aunt Agatha frowned at her she knew she'd gone too far.

"Why all these questions?"

"I was just curious, that's all. Now that everybody is nervous."

"I don't know." The expression on Aunt Agatha's face made her realize that Agatha knew what she was up to. The only thing she could do was get out of there fast.

"Well, I should go. I've got to help *Mamm* with some things."

"You only just got here. Aren't you going to wait for the teakettle to boil?"

"Oh, yes, sorry." She sat back down remembering she had said she would stay for a cup of hot tea.

"And how's young Dean?"

"Dean is good."

"Your *mudder* said you were getting friendlier with him."

"We were, but now we're not."

"Oh, that was fast—you were, and then you weren't?"

"That's right. That's how we young people are these days."

Agatha chortled and shook a finger at her. "You took the words right out of my mouth."

"That's because I knew you were about to say that." Rebecca grinned at her Aunt.

"You really should give him a chance."

"I gave him one. Sort of two. I really did and it didn't work out too well."

"Why? What happened?" Agatha leaned forward.

"It's just that … I guess I wanted to feel special and he made me feel I was just another girl. And now he tells me he wants to get married soon and I get the feeling that just anybody will do for him. He'd be happy with anyone."

"Did you talk to him about it?"

"Actually, we did have a conversation about it. And I don't think it worked out very well." She told Agatha about May and April. "I mean, what would you have done if *Onkel*

Alfred had gone out with your worst enemy?"

"Those girls are hardly your worst enemy."

"Okay let me find another way to say it. What would you have done if *Onkel* Alfred had asked out the woman in the community that you liked the very least?"

She shook her head. "I wouldn't have liked it one little bit."

"You see what I mean now?"

Agatha stared at Rebecca a few moments before she spoke. "Sometimes I forget what it was like to be a young girl."

"Do you still think I should give him a second chance? Or, rather, a third one?"

"It's what you think that counts."

"I'm confused because everybody has so many different opinions. It's hard to know what to think sometimes."

"You're the one who has to live with your decisions, so maybe you should take a few weeks to yourself and stop listening to other people. Everyone would run your life if you let them. Sometimes you just have to stand up and speak your mind even if it's going against what everyone else thinks. As long as you're not going against *Gott* or his word. What you have to do is listen to *Gott's* small voice in amongst all the other voices."

"Good idea. *Denke,* Aunt Agatha."

"Let Him be your guide. Go somewhere quiet and be alone with *Gott* and listen to the promptings that come from deep within your heart."

"Maybe I'll do that. In fact, that's the most sensible thing I've heard for a long time."

Aunt Agatha gave a little giggle.

"That must be what great aunts are for."

Agatha continued stroking her cat. "You know, there was a time in my life when I considered being a midwife."

"Really?"

THE AMISH WIDOWER'S PROMISE

"Jah, I think you got the liking of it from me. You take after me."

"What stopped you?"

A giant tabby cat took a flying leap and landed on Agatha's lap next to the other one. The suddenness of the movement scared Rebecca half to death, but Agatha didn't flinch. She simply started stroking the new cat, who'd pushed the other one off her lap. The first one who'd been on her lap slinked away. "Alfred didn't want me to be away from home."

"Ah, I see. That's understandable. It does take a lot of time and nights away from the family. Did he object to you doing it before you were married?"

"I first thought about it after I had our first child. Before that I never gave it two thoughts, but the midwife I had was so lovely and so comforting that I thought I'd like to help other women. She really had a way about her. And then, well, I got busy with my family and got over the feeling."

"I never knew that you wanted to do it."

"My *grossmammi* was a midwife."

"Really? I didn't know that."

"It runs in our family. Didn't your *vadder* tell you that?"

"*Nee,* he didn't."

"She and my *grossdaddi* were the ones who started the community in Pleasant Valley."

"That's right. I remember hearing something about that going way back, but I didn't know there were any other midwives in the family. I thought it was just me."

"There you go. See what you find out when you visit me?"

"*Jah.*"

Rebecca had a pleasant cup of tea and a piece of cream-filled sponge cake with Aunt Agatha and then headed home. Knowing a little more of her family history confirmed she should continue with midwifery.

She would have to find a man who appreciated her important job. Or maybe, and perhaps better still, would she be happier without a man, just as Marilyn had been without one?

CHAPTER 21

MONTHS PASSED and all Rebecca could do was keep away from both Dean and Jacob. Neither man was happy with her.

The anniversary of Beth and William's death arrived. It had been three years since the dreadful accident.

Mary was at the bishop's house having hot tea with Hannah and Rebecca while Rebecca's younger brothers were entertaining Lois.

"It's been three years since Beth and William have been gone."

"It seems like only a year," Hannah said.

"Rebecca, will you come to the graveyard with me? I went by myself before now, but this time, since you were there at Lois's birth, I'd like you to come too. Freda will watch Lois while we go."

Rebecca nodded. The two of them shared a secret that Hannah didn't know. The truth of Lois's birth; that she was Mary's child and not Beth's like everyone thought. "I'll come. When is it?"

"Today."

"Oh. You want to go now?"

"*Jah.* I'll just have to stop by home and leave Lois with Freda."

"Sure. I've got no appointments today."

AFTER THEY STOPPED BACK at Mary's house, Mary talked with Freda and then cut some flowers to take to the graves.

Leaving Mary's house, Rebecca said, "I've

never visited anyone at a graveyard. I mean, I know they're not really there. It's just their bodies."

"I know, of course, but Beth was my closest friend and I feel closer to her when I'm there. Lois would've had such a good life with them, and the funny thing is I never would've got to know Samuel if she hadn't died. He seemed so arrogant and then I found out it was just a shield. Just a covering he showed to the world."

"So, he's not extremely confident?"

"*Jah,* he is, but that's different from being arrogant."

"Yeah, I guess you're right." Rebecca didn't know whether she wanted to go to the graveyard and look at all those mossy headstones overgrown with weeds. Then she thought about the latest gossip. "Did you hear April is getting married?"

Mary glanced over at her. "Really?"

"That's what I heard. I overheard *Dat*

telling *Mamm*. I think it will be announced at the next meeting."

"That is a surprise. It just goes to show there's someone for everyone. I only hope the man she's marrying knows her very well."

"Everyone's got faults I guess, but I know what you mean." Rebecca giggled about all the things April and May had gotten up to in the past. "Maybe it was a good idea to separate the twins."

"It sounds like it."

When they got to the graveyard they saw another Amish buggy.

"Do we know them?" Mary asked.

Rebecca looked around for the person who owned the buggy and eventually she saw Jacob in the middle of the graveyard heading back to the buggy. "It's Jacob."

"I'm not feeling sociable at the moment. Can you talk with him while I tie the horse?" Mary asked.

"Sure." Rebecca got out of the buggy, wondering what she'd say to him since she knew he would've been at his wife's grave. Over the past months, they'd seen each other at every gathering and function the community had. Sometimes Rebecca found herself wishing she'd accepted his proposal because now, since she'd rejected him, she knew he'd never risk another rejection by asking her a second time. She was relieved when he waved and smiled. For some reason, she had thought he might be in a sullen mood.

"This is a surprise," he said as he drew closer.

With a quick look back at Mary, she explained, "This is the anniversary of some friends of ours who died in an accident. They were husband and wife."

He nodded. "I come here sometimes. I find it peaceful."

Rebecca nodded and wondered if at times he had wished he'd died with Mona. It can't have been easy to be the spouse left behind. "I'm sorry we had that misunderstanding a while back."

"Me too. Mona obviously thought highly of you, so we should be friends—better friends than we are."

It confirmed that there could never be anything between them because he was always bringing up Mona's name. She'd always be there with them, if they married, and, as Timothy had pointed out, she'd never be the woman of the household. That job had been taken already by Anne.

"I'm sorry about your friends," he said, touching her quickly and lightly on her arm.

"*Denke.* It was a shock to everyone. Beth was best of friends with Mary and Karen."

"I didn't make the connection at first. Beth is Samuel's *schweschder, jah?*"

"That's right."

"I don't think he'll ever get over her

death, but he certainly brightened up when he married Mary."

"They say the right woman will do that."

He smiled and looked down. Then he looked up and their eyes locked. Something passed between them like a bolt of energy. "Would you consider coming for dinner one night soon?"

She felt like a drop of sunlight was shining into a deep, dark place. "I'd like that." It wasn't a date, but it was a start.

"Tomorrow night? If you're not busy."

"I'm doing nothing. I'll bring the dessert."

He raised his hands. *"Nee,* Anne wouldn't hear of it. Shall I collect you around six?"

She could barely keep the smile from her face. He was collecting her, so it was becoming more like a date. "Fine."

With perfect timing, Mary joined them and greeted Jacob. Then after a few polite words were exchanged, Jacob left them and

Mary and Rebecca went to find Beth and William's side-by-side graves.

Once they heard Jacob's horse and buggy trotting away, Mary said, "What's going on? What happened back there? And don't even try to say, 'nothing.' I could feel the sparks flying."

Rebecca giggled. "He invited me to his *haus* tomorrow night for dinner."

Mary stopped walking and pulled on Rebecca's arm. "And ... you better have said yes?"

Rebecca nodded. "I did. He's collecting me at six."

They both started walking again. "That's better than you driving there," Mary said.

"That's what I thought. It's more of a date, isn't it?"

"*Jah.*"

They stopped at the graves, and Rebecca remembered the day of the funeral and the sadness in the air after such a loss to the community. Everyone had been so sad for Lois, whom they all had regarded an orphan. Rebecca didn't want to tell Mary what to do, but she sure hoped that Lois wouldn't believe the lie and then later find out the truth. Rebecca was certain Mary and Samuel should tell the truth to the community now and suffer the consequences, and then Lois would grow up knowing the truth of who her real mother was. As it stood, only she, Mary and Samuel knew that Mary was Lois's real mother, not Beth.

Mary kneeled down by the grave and closed her eyes. Rebecca wondered whether she was in silent communication with God asking what to do about the situation. Rebecca joined her and kneeled beside her. Rebecca prayed for Mary, Samuel and Lois, that all would be well with the secret they carried. Rebecca's father had taught her that lies were a burden that someone carried, like bearing a heavy sack of wheat on one's back.

Still, she'd already made her thoughts known to Mary and that was all she could do.

A few minutes later, Rebecca sat back on her heels and opened her eyes and saw that Mary had hers open, too.

"*Denke* for coming with me, Rebecca."

"Any time."

"I feel so sad because she never had *kinner* of her own. I feel guilty sometimes for having my second one." Mary rubbed her tummy.

"She had Lois. Lois was exactly the same as her child. Well, she was for the months they had her. You gave that gift to her."

"I know. It was hard at the time to pass her over, but I'm glad I did. Now I have Lois back, and I wouldn't if they hadn't died." She stared back at the grave.

"Life's funny sometimes, but you can't feel guilty for being happy."

Mary looked over at her and the gentle breeze blew some loose strands of red hair across her face. She pushed them away. "Is that what I'm doing?"

"I think so. Just be happy with what you have and don't think about anything that makes you sad. There's plenty I can think about that makes me want to cry, but you can't dwell on it. Sometimes when you look around you can only see suffering in the world. We have to grab hold of our happiness and appreciate it. You've had your fair share of hardships, and now look at you."

"I've been blessed in so many ways." She looked back at the graves. "I'll see you again someday, Beth and William." Then Mary stood. "Are you ready to go?"

"*Jah.* Let's go."

CHAPTER 22

FOR THE NEXT TWENTY-FOUR HOURS, all Rebecca could think of was her dinner at Jacob's house. Nothing would make her happier than to marry Jacob. He was a real man and despite what her brother said, she knew Jacob was the kind of person to find a way to keep both women in his life happy. Surely her proper place would be as the woman of the household.

She caught herself thinking too far into the future and cautioned herself not to get her hopes up. He'd mentioned being her friend, so what if that was all he wanted, just friendship?

JACOB HAD SHOWN her over the last few months that he had all the qualities she wanted in a man. Of course, it wasn't ideal to marry someone who'd been married, or a man so many years older, but she preferred that choice over marrying someone like Dean, who wasn't mature.

She wanted—and hoped that Jacob would want—more than just a friendship, and for that reason she took special care over her appearance.

Her lilac dress was the one she chose because every time she wore it she received compliments. People said the mauve highlights brought out her complexion and enhanced her dark eyes.

Her mother had a huge smile on her face when she told her where she was going that night, and her father was out somewhere doing church business. He often visited people as well as having people over to the house.

When she heard a buggy, she said goodbye to her mother and brothers, grabbed her black over bonnet and placed it on her head, took hold of her coat and headed out the door.

"Behave yourself," she heard her mother say as she closed the door. She laughed, hoping Jacob hadn't heard her ill-timed remark. It was something her mother often said to her young brothers.

She reached the buggy before Jacob had a chance to get out. Then she saw his shaved face. It was a sign he no longer considered himself to be married. The single men were the only ones who shaved. The married men grew their beards, and only shaved above their lips.

"You ... you've shaved." She couldn't stop

herself from saying it, and wondered if she should've kept quiet and pretended not to notice. As she climbed into the buggy her eyes were fixed on how handsome a face had been hidden by the beard.

"I have. Are you ready?"

"Jah." She spread her coat over her knees. "Did you cook dinner?"

"Nee, Anne did it. Thankfully. You wouldn't want to eat what I cooked."

"What are we eating?" she asked, saying whatever came to mind because she felt awkward about having mentioned the beard.

"I believe we have braised turkey and roasted vegetables. I'm sure there's more, but that's all I can think about because that's my favorite." He chuckled.

"Good to know." She'd have to remember that. Now that his beard was shaved off, she worried that other girls would be interested in him. That meant she had to put her best foot forward tonight, and make a good impression. "How is Anne enjoying it here in Pleasant Valley?"

"She already has more friends here than where we were before. She's so much happier."

"Good. It seems like it was a good move all around."

"And how is your job? Delivering plenty of *bopplis?*"

"Really good. I'm learning more and more as the weeks go by, with every *boppli* that's delivered."

"It's good to have an interest such as that."

"*Jah*, it's more of a career." She hoped he understood that, if things were to get serious between them.

"Very true."

REBECCA GREETED Anne when she got to the house, and then Anne showed them to the dining room.

When Rebecca walked in, she saw that there was a table set for two. "Anne, you're not joining us?"

"Not today. I ate earlier and I will have Micah to look after."

When Anne hurried out of the room, Rebecca looked at Jacob. "You didn't tell me it was just us."

He stared at her with his soft hazel brown eyes. "Would you have come?"

"I would."

He pulled out a chair for her and she sat in it, then he sat opposite. He cleared his throat. "I don't know if you've forgiven me for what happened after—"

"It's in the past. Let's leave it there."

Anne had already sliced the turkey and other roasted meats, and had everything laid out in the center of the table. "This is a feast," said Rebecca as she looked over the many choices.

"Hope you're hungry."

"I always am, it seems. I love food."

When they had placed their selections on their plates, they closed their eyes for the silent prayer to give thanks for the food. Once they opened their eyes, they heard Micah's whimpers from a distant room.

"That's as much as he cries."

"He's such a lovely *bu*."

After they had a couple of mouthfuls of food, Jacob cleared his throat. "How's Dean?"

"I don't know. We don't really talk much these days. I heard that April's getting married."

A hint of a smile touched his lips. "That's good."

"That's right. Sorry I mentioned her. I forgot what happened." She shook her head remembering the incident April had accused Jacob of.

"Forgot? I wish I could. And, just for the record, nothing happened."

"I know that." She laughed. "I meant I had

forgotten about what she said, and all that fuss that was created. I've had her do things to me, but nothing as bad as what she did to you."

He inhaled deeply. "I was believed, so I'm happy about that."

"This food is really good. Do you eat like this every night?"

"This is a special meal, but Anne is a very good cook."

Rebecca nodded. "I can tell."

"What about you?"

"I'm okay. I had to cook from a young age with all my brothers, and I'm used to cooking large meals."

"You've got a big family. How do you feel about having one yourself some day?"

"A big family?"

He'd just popped a forkful of meat into his mouth, so he nodded.

"*Jah,* I'd like to have many *kinner,* but then it would be hard for me to work as much."

He placed his elbows on the table. "Which is more important, delivering *bopplis* or having your own family?"

"Hmm, if I had to choose one or the other, I'd choose my own. That's not a hard choice to make." She reached over for the bowl of beans and spooned more onto her plate. Remembering she'd rejected him more than once, she knew she had to somehow let him know she was interested.

"One thing I have to say …"

She leaned forward, hoping he might propose marriage. It was too soon, she knew, but she still hoped. "What's that?"

"I am sorry that I was rude to you about April and May."

She frowned, thinking of April and May as months, and then she realized he meant the twins. "Oh them."

"I wasn't appreciative about you encouraging May to confess what April had been up to, concocting the lies. I mean, I was appreciative to get out of it with my reputation still intact, but I should've thanked you for what you did. Instead, I only saw the negative side."

"I guess I was deceitful the way I went about it. You were right about that."

"I know, but you did that for me. I am grateful. *Denke.*"

She smiled. "I'll accept your apology, even though it is very late, and I'll also accept your thanks."

He gave a chuckle. "That makes me feel better."

"Good." It wasn't a proposal, but they were moving to a better place and putting past difference behind them. Rebecca was happy with that for the moment.

CHAPTER 23

AFTER DINNER, they moved into the living room.

"Would you like coffee, or anything else?" he asked.

Anne was nowhere to be seen and Rebecca assumed she'd gone to bed. "I couldn't fit anything else in even if I wanted to. I enjoyed the meal so much."

"I'll be sure to tell Anne."

"*Jah,* please do."

They chatted for a while and then it came time for him to take her home. Rebecca hoped that this would be when he'd say something to reveal any feelings he had for her.

They were halfway home, before he spoke at all. "I'm glad we've become friends again, Rebecca."

Again, with the friends thing. She didn't know what to say; she wished she could let him know she wanted more, but there was nothing right she could say. He had to be fond of her, otherwise he wouldn't have shaved and invited her for dinner and if she rushed things it could ruin everything. "I'm glad too."

"Maybe we could see more of each other?" he glanced over at her.

She looked back at him and couldn't keep the smile from her face. *"Jah,* I'd like to see you other than at the meetings." Now she felt silly because he was saying everything and she was just agreeing.

"Or, we could get married." His words

were said almost under his breath, but Rebecca couldn't mistake what she'd heard.

"What?" she almost screeched, caught off-guard even though it was what she'd hoped for.

"I'm sorry, Rebecca, forgive me. It was a stupid thing to say, especially now that we've mended our bridges and gotten along better."

"You have feelings for me?"

He took his eyes off the road as he slowed his horse to a gentle walk, and gazed at her. "I've had feelings for you for a long time. Since not long after I moved here."

"I didn't know."

"Now, I guess I've ruined our friendship."

"*Nee,* Jacob, you haven't. I have feelings for you too."

His lips turned upward at the corners. "More than friendship?"

She nodded. "I do."

"Then, what do you say to the question I

asked before?"

"Which one was that?" Rebecca thought she'd never hastily answer another question without thinking of the confusion with Dean and the big mix-up.

He chuckled. "The one where I asked you to marry me?"

"I'm not certain I heard properly. Can you ask it again?"

His eyes twinkled by the light of the moon, and he stopped his buggy on the side of the quiet road. He turned toward her and took her hand. "Rebecca, will you marry me?"

Now she had what she wanted and she couldn't have been happier. She no longer feared she'd be compared to his late wife because from what she'd been told about her and from when she'd met her, she'd come to love Mona too. They would've been good friends. She stared into his eyes, wanting to remember this romantic moment forever.

Dean wasn't right; there could be marriage and romance. With her free hand, she wiped a tear away from her eye.

"I'm making you cry," he said, pulling out his handkerchief and handing it to her. "I hope they're good tears."

She dried her eyes and sniffed. "They are. If we marry, what would you think about me carrying on with my—"

"I'd be upset if you stopped."

"But who—?"

"We'll move out of the rental *haus* and buy another. I'll build a *grossdaddi haus* on for Anne, if there isn't one already. I'm ready to buy right now. Anne can live with us, but not *with* us. She'll be pleased to help out when you're working."

"Oh, so you've got this—"

"All figured out? *Jah*, I've been thinking on it for some time." He leaned closer to her. "I've thought of little else, to tell you the truth."

His breath from his whispered words tickled her neck and she giggled with delight that all her questions had been answered. "It would make me happy to marry you, Jacob."

"You will?"

"*Jah,* I will." He pulled her closer to him and she rested her head on his strong manly shoulder. Right there under the moonlight, she knew she'd found the one God had designed just for her. Jacob was understanding and he knew it would be better for their young family if his sister wasn't living in the house with them, even though she would be part of their family life. And he fully supported the idea of his wife's midwifery career. Their start had been unusual, but they'd eventually found their way. Rebecca was glad he didn't mention Mona's promise, but she knew they were both thinking Mona had been right in choosing her to marry Jacob.

. . .

"I'M SO excited I want to shout it from a mountaintop. I just want to tell everyone. What do you say I turn around and we tell Anne? She'll be beside herself with excitement."

Rebecca laughed. "Okay." As he turned the buggy around, she was a little disappointed her parents wouldn't hear of it first, but it made sense to do it this way. Then they could tell her parents when he took her home. Besides, now that she was getting married, she had to learn to compromise and small things like this were a good place to start. "I do hope she's happy."

"She will be."

When the buggy drew closer to the house, they saw Anne through the kitchen window washing the dishes. Jacob wasted no time jumping down from the buggy and he immediately rushed to Rebecca's side as she too climbed down.

He took her hand and as he pushed the

door open, Anne said, "That was fast." Then she saw Rebecca. "Oh, did you forget something?"

Jacob said, "We have some news and I wanted you to be the first to know."

Her eyes widened.

"Rebecca has agreed to marry me."

Anne squealed, hugged Jacob and then wrapped her arms around Rebecca. "This is good news. Shall I put more coffee on?"

"Nee, we have to tell Rebecca's parents now." He looked at Rebecca. "Don't we?"

"Jah, we should." Rebecca giggled, feeling more happiness than she'd ever felt before.

"I told Rebecca my plans of getting a *haus* with a *grossdaddi haus* for you."

"Jah, I won't intrude on your lives. I'll be there when you need me. I'll look after all your *kinner* because I don't have any of my own. I'm happy to play as big or as small a part in their lives as you want."

"Rebecca will need your help, won't you?" He looked at Rebecca with a proud smile.

"*Jah*, Anne, I will. Jacob and I have agreed that I will continue my job."

"*Jah*, and so you should," Anne said.

"*Denke*, Anne. Everything will work out perfectly." She stepped forward and hugged Anne again.

"It will."

TWENTY MINUTES and another buggy ride later, they arrived at Rebecca's house.

"I hope they're happy, considering I'm older and have already been married. They might be thinking of someone else for you."

"Stop worrying. They'll be pleased."

Rebecca pushed the door open and called out to her mother and father as she stepped into the house with Jacob by her side.

"How was the dinner?" her mother asked. Then she looked up from her mending. "Oh!

Good evening, Jacob. I didn't realize you'd come in with Rebecca."

"Dinner was good," Rebecca said trying her best to keep from laughing.

"We have some news," Jacob said.

Rebecca's father looked up from his newspaper and peered at them. "What is it?"

"Rebecca has agreed to marry me."

Her father looked at them, saying nothing while her smiling mother quickly stood, congratulated them and hugged them.

"What's going on?" Timothy asked, coming out of the kitchen.

"Seems that my only *dochder* has decided to leave our *haus*." Bishop Elmer's face softened into a smile.

"Is that right." Timothy pointed at them. "The two of you?"

Jacob nodded while Rebecca said, *"Jah,* we're getting married."

"When?"

"I don't know." She looked up at Jacob. "Do we?"

"Not yet. I'll have to discuss times with your father."

"Can I have your room when you go?" Timothy asked Rebecca.

Everyone laughed.

Timothy shrugged his shoulders. "You try living five to a room." He moved forward and shook Jacob's hand and then hugged his sister. "This is a surprise—a very good one."

Jacob said to Bishop Elmer, "Can we have a talk about this tomorrow and finalize a date?"

"Sure. How about just after lunch?"

"Perfect. I'll be here. Well, it's late, and I'm sorry to be delivering news to you at this late hour."

Hannah said, "I'm so glad you did. Good news is always welcome."

Rebecca walked Jacob outside and back to his buggy. "I'm so happy, Jacob."

He took hold of her hand. "Me too. We will have a good life together. I'm glad you overlooked our age difference."

"I haven't even given it a second thought." She laughed. "I didn't think tonight would turn out like this."

"Me either, but I'm glad it did." He raised her hand to his mouth and softly pressed his lips against the back of her hand.

THAT NIGHT, Rebecca tossed and turned and couldn't sleep. She kept imagining her life with Jacob, and becoming Micah's step-mother. Just when the morning sun peeped over the horizon, she drifted into a dream. She and Mona were walking side-by-side along a riverbank path. No words were spoken, but Rebecca could sense Mona was happy.

They approached a sun-dappled clear-ing, and Rebecca saw Jacob sitting there on a picnic blanket with Micah on his lap. Mona stopped and watched "her men" for a moment, and then made eye contact with Rebecca. Mona smiled at her, gently nudged her toward the clearing, turned around, and walked back the way they'd come.

Rebecca watched her until she went around a curve and disappeared behind the bushes that lined the trail. As Rebecca turned back to walk toward Jacob and Micah, she awoke. She lay there awhile, feeling at peace and she again thanked God for just the right man for her.

I hope you enjoyed *The Amish Widower's Promise.*

If you'd like to be notified of my new releases and special offers, be sure to add your email at the Newsletter section of my website:

SamanthaPriceAuthor.com

Blessings,

Samantha Price

AMISH WOMEN OF PLEASANT VALLEY

Book 1 The Amish Woman and Her Last Hope

Book 2 The Amish Woman and Her Secret Baby

Book 3 The Amish Widower's Promise

Book 4 The Amish Visitors

Book 5 The Amish Dreamer

Book 6 The Amish School Teacher

Book 7 Amish Baby Blessing

Book 8 Amish Christmas Wedding

Amish Women of Pleasant Valley Boxed Set Books 1 - 4

Amish Women of Pleasant Valley Boxed Set Books 5 - 8

ABOUT SAMANTHA PRICE

USA Today Bestselling author, Samantha Price, wrote stories from a young age, but it wasn't until later in life that she took up writing full time. Formally an artist, she exchanged her paintbrush for the computer and, many best-selling book series later, has never looked back.

Samantha is happiest on her computer lost in the world of her characters. She is best known for the Amish Bonnet Sisters series and the Expectant Amish Widows series.

www.SamanthaPriceAuthor.com

Samantha loves to hear from her readers. Connect with her at:

samantha@samanthapriceauthor.com
www.facebook.com/SamanthaPriceAuthor
Follow Samantha Price on BookBub
Twitter @ AmishRomance
Instagram - SamanthaPriceAuthor

CPSIA information can be obtained
at www.ICGtesting.com
Printed in the USA
LVHW080004220621
690817LV00024B/966